THE TRUCE WILLIAMS STORY

DAVID SURLES

THE TRUCE WILLIAMS STORY

iUniverse books may be ordered through booksellers or by contacting:

iUniverse
1663 Liberty Drive
Bloomington, IN 47403
www.iuniverse.com
1-800-Authors (1-800-288-4677)

ISBN: 978-1-5320-8002-9 (sc)
ISBN: 978-1-5320-8003-6 (e)

Library of Congress Control Number: 2019912036

Print information available on the last page.

iUniverse rev. date: 09/24/2019

CHAPTER 1

As the two leaders walked toward a large dumpster to discuss the peace treaty between the two rival street organizations, Pimp said to Black, "What's up, Black? How's the street life treating you?"

"Shit, Pimp, I'm just trying to hold my own and duck the bullets coming out of the barrels of your boys' guns at the same time. This shit is scandalous, but, my nigga, I can't complain. Besides, a gangster can't live but two lives."

"What's that, my nigga?" asked Pimp.

"That of a lover and that of a legend," said Black with a big smile on his face.

"Damn, Black," said Pimp. "You got a hell of a mouthpiece."

"They don't call me Black the Mack for nothing."

"Well, Black," said Pimp, "with all of the warring going on between us, money has been kind of slow for the last couple of months."

"Yeah, Pimp, you're so right," replied Black. "And those damn foreigners are sucking our neighborhood dry. Our people have been spending their money at those Jewish stores for the past six years, and the Jews haven't done anything for our community. We have got to do something about this."

"But what?" responded Pimp.

"Well, my nigger, if they don't want to give our people anything, we will just have to make them pay for using our neighborhood."

"What if they don't want to pay us, Black?" asked Pimp.

"That will just be fine," answered Black. "We just have to let their store accidentally burn down."

"Black, man, you know what they call that shit? They call that shit extortion!" Pimp exclaimed.

"That's not called extortion," Black calmly said to Pimp.

"Then what in the hell is it called?"

"It's called using what you got to get what you want."

"Okay, Black, I'm down for whatever," said Pimp while extending his hand toward Black.

Black shook Pimp's hand with a peculiar handshake that only a person from the hood could understand.

Pimp said to Black with a serious look on his face, "What up, nigger? From this day forth, you and your boys don't have to worry about me and my boys shooting up any more of your spots, if you can promise me and my boys the same in return."

"It's a promise," Black said. "I give you my word. Word is bond, and bond is life."

"Before my word shall fail, I promise you, Black, I will give my life."

Shortly after the two agreed on the peace treaty, there was a noise that started to come from the dumpster.

"Black, you hear that shit?" said Pimp with a disturbed voice while pulling a very large gun from underneath his shirt.

Black pulled an even larger pistol from underneath his shirt. The two of them crept toward the dumpster, and Black slid the lid back on the dumpster.

"It's probably a cat," Pimp said while they looked inside of the dumpster to see what was making the strange noise. "Black, there's nothing but trash in here. Man, this shit stinks."

"There goes that noise again, Pimp. Did you hear it?"

"Yeah, Black, I heard it. It's coming from that cardboard box."

"Well, Pimp, stick your hand in there and open the box, man."

"You crazy as hell! It might be a big-ass cat in that box, Black. If you want to see what's in that box, you will have to go in it your damn self!"

"Damn! Pimp, you're supposed to be gangster! And you're scared to open a box? Watch out, man. Let me open the box." Black reached for the box with his left hand while pointing the gun toward the box with his right. Black opened the box. "It's a baby! Pimp, it's a baby!" Black pulled the baby out of the box. The baby was crying.

"It's a little girl," said Pimp.

"Hold her for a minute, Pimp, while I take my shirt off and wrap it around her."

"Black, this is a black baby. I wonder what sister would put her baby inside a dumpster."

"To tell you the truth, Pimp, more than likely the sister was a dope addict, and she probably got tired of carrying the baby around with her."

"So, Black, what are we going to do with her?"

"Well, my girl, Pam, wants a little girl. She can't have any more children—we already have two boys, and to be honest with you, Pimp, I bet having a daughter would be cool as hell!"

Pimp said, "You need to hold up, my nigga. Both of us found her. She's just as much mine as yours. Besides, I have a little boy and a little girl, and me and my baby, Mechell, would love to have another little girl around the crib."

"I tell you what, Pimp," said Black while holding the little baby in his arms. "She's both of ours, and she will have two fathers and two mothers."

"Damn!" said Pimp. "She's going to have a lot of love."

"One thing's for sure," said Black. "She don't have to worry about anyone messing with her. Well, what are we going to name her?"

"How about Sonya?" Pimp offered.

"Sonya? Hell no! Pimp, we have to give her a name that means something," said Black.

"How about Christy? That sounds like a good name. What do you think about it, Black?"

"Christy!" repeated Black with excitement. "Have you been burning some of that Mary Jane, nigga? You've got to be high, Pimp! Christy sounds like a name for a white girl."

"Well, all right, nigga," Pimp said. "Have you come up with a name yet?"

"You know that I have," said Black with a big smile, showing his pearly white teeth. "Truce Williams."

"What the hell is a truce?" asked Pimp.

"Truce means peace," answered Black. "The reason we call her Truce is because she will be the link that links the Vice Lords and the Disciples together. Her name will forever remind us of the peace treaty that we agreed on."

The little baby began crying.

"She must be hungry. I am going to stop by the store and buy some milk, diapers, and baby food," Black said.

Pimp pulled a large roll of money out of his pocket. "Here's three hundred dollars for Truce."

"Thanks, Pimp," Black said while putting the money in his pocket as they walked toward the cars, which were heavily guarded by their foot soldiers.

As Pimp and Black made it to their cars, Black was greeted by his right-hand man, Dirty Left. "Oh, gangster, what's that in your arms? A six-pack?"

Upon Dirty Left's remark, Black and Pimp looked at each other and began to laugh. "Hell no, Left," said Black. "This is my little daughter."

"Your little daughter?" echoed Left with surprise. "Black, you don't have a daughter—you only have two sons."

"I will explain it to Left when we get to the flat," Black said to Pimp. "Here, Left." Black handed Left the little baby, which was wrapped up in his leather jacket. The jacket said "Disciples" on the back of it in large blue letters. The little baby looked even smaller in the hands of Left, who was a six-foot-eleven albino and the hardest-fighting soldier in the Disciples besides Black. Left had hands the size of baseball gloves. The reason why he was called Dirty Left was because he had a left hook that was known to break the jaw of anyone who fell victim to it. Besides Left's dangerous hook, he had a very deep love in his heart for little children, and Left often punched grown-ups in his neighborhood who took advantage of little children.

"Well, Pimp," said Black, "I will holla at you later. I have to go to the store and get Truce some milk before she busts me and Left's eardrums with all of that noise."

Pimp replied, "Okay."

"You be easy, Pimp," said Left while closing the door of Black's blue 1957 Chevy.

CHAPTER 2

Black and Left arrived at Ms. Suzy May's grocery store, which was the only black-owned grocery store on the west side of Chicago. They were greeted by Ms. Suzy, who had ran outside after seeing Black's blue Chevy pull up in the small parking lot.

"Hey, baby!" said Ms. Suzy while approaching Black's car.

Left grimaced.

"Damn! Left, you act like you scared of Ms. Suzy or something," Black said. "Man, if I were you, I would have to tap that ass!"

Ms. Suzy was short at four feet eleven. She was a dark-skinned sister. At forty-eight years of age, Suzy had a body that put twenty-year-old sisters to shame. She had a figure like an Egyptian goddess.

"Hey, Black," said Suzy. "Where's my baby Left at?"

"He's right here beside me, holding my little daughter." As Black got out of the car, he said to Ms. Suzy, "Suzy May, I need to get some diapers, milk, and baby food for Truce."

"Boy," said Ms. Suzy while getting inside the car with Left, "you'd better take your ass on in there. Hell, long as I've known your ass, you're like family. Tell Nicky I said get up off her ass and serve you." Nicky was Suzy's daughter, and she was only nineteen but looked so much like her mom that they could pass for twins.

After Black made it into the store, Ms. Suzy turned her head around and said to Left, "I thought that you were going to come over last night and play some cards with us."

"I was really looking forward to coming over last night, but something came up, and I had to handle a little business."

"Yeah, you probably were with one of your bitches."

"Who, me? Naw, Suzy May, you know that I don't like dogs. You *are* referring to a dog, aren't you? Because I know that a lady of your caliber would not dare label another sister as a bitch. Besides, I don't have a woman."

"Nigga, I don't want to hear that shit. I've been trying to give you this ass for over two years now. You make me think that you're scared of pussy or something."

"Waah, waah!"

"See there, Suzy May? Look at what you've done. You've upset Truce, talking that bullshit!"

"I'm sorry, Left. Let me hold her."

Left handed the crying baby to Suzy.

"Shh, shh," said Suzy to the little baby.

By the time that Suzy got the baby to be quiet, Black walked out of the store with three bags in his hand. "Suzy May?"

"What the hell do you want, Black?"

"Don't you and Left be kissing and shit over my little girl."

"Black, you can kiss my ass. See, you think that you are slick, but you've been in the damn store for thirty minutes. It don't take you that damn long to get some milk, diapers, and baby food."

"Ha! Suzy May, you're crazy as hell."

"See, Black, you're laughing, but if I catch you fuckin' around with my daughter, I'm going to put that thirty-eight on your black ass!" Suzy handed the baby back over to Left while kissing him on the side of the jaw.

Black said, "Suzy, move out of the damn way so that I can put these bags in the back seat."

"Nigga, who in the hell do you think that you talking to?"

"He's talking to your ass," said Left.

"That's right, Left. Put her smart ass in check."

"Black, you've got me fucked up. Don't no nigga put me in check. And Left, you riding with that bullshit? See, y'all niggers ain't fooling me. I have been trying to give Left this pussy for two whole years. The motherfucker acts like he's scared of pussy, but I know what it is. Y'all are fucking!"

Black and Left laughed. Black said, "Woman, you've got a very dirty mouth."

"Mama, Mama," said Suzy's daughter. "Somebody wants you on the telephone."

"Who is it, baby?"

"Some woman. Hey, Black."

"Hey, Nicky."

"All right now, Black. I done told you about my baby."

"Suzy, you know that I wouldn't mess with Nicky. She's like a little sister to me."

"Well, I guess that I need to go and answer this phone. Y'all take care, all right?"

"Suzy, you do the same," said Black as he drove away. "Yo, Left."

"Yeah, what's up, Black?"

"Where do want me to drop you off? At home?"

"Naw, Black, drop me off at my sister's house."

"Which one? Shay or Roxanne?"

"Roxanne's house, Black, so that I can pick up my car."

"Well, Left, we're here," said Black while pulling up to the parking lot of the South Side's housing projects. "Oh, Left, I want you to bring Truce in the house for me while I grab these bags."

"Cool, Black, no problem."

"Left, you can go ahead and take Truce in the house. I'll be right behind you just as soon as I get these bags. You can give Truce to Pam, if you're in a hurry."

"I am going to stay over with you for about thirty minutes. Besides, you haven't told me where you got this cute little baby from."

Left knocked on the door, and Pam opened it. "Left! Why are you knocking on the door? You'd better come on in. Left, is that your little baby?"

"No, Pam. I thought that you and Black had another baby."

Pam gave an artificial smile, trying not to expose her shock to Left.

Black walked through the door. "What's up, baby?"

"I don't know," responded Pam with concern. "But after you put those grocery bags down, you need to come over here and explain to me what the hell Left is talking about. He says that this is your baby."

Black laughed. "I will explain it to you after I fix Truce a bottle of milk." Truce began to cry. "Hold up, baby. Daddy's on the way." After Black filled up the bottle with milk, he walked over to Left, who was sitting on the couch. "Left, let me have my little girl."

"Sure, Black," said Left while handing the baby to Black.

Black gently put the bottle inside of the crying baby's mouth. The baby immediately sucked on the bottle.

Pam said, "Baby, don't you have something to tell me?"

"Oh, Pam, my precious, I almost forgot. Today, Pimp and I were discussing settling differences in a reasonable manner. While doing this on the side of an old building, we heard a noise coming from the dumpster, so we looked inside of the dumpster to see what was making the noise. We found Truce inside of a box that was inside of the dumpster."

"Damn! That's fucked up," said Left.

Pam said, "Poor baby. What are we going to do with her? Can we keep her?"

"That's exactly what Pimp and I decided to do."

"So, Black, what you're telling me is that I'm a godfather?"

"Yes, Left. You're Truce's godfather."

Pam said, "Let me hold my daughter." Black passed the baby to Pam. "Black, what in the hell are you doing with this shirt wrapped around her? You mean to tell me that you went to the store and forgot to get some diapers?"

"Naw, I got some diapers and some baby food. It's in those bags."

"Well, hand it to me, baby." Black walked over to the table to get the diapers.

Left said, "Yo, Black, I've got to step. I will blow at you tomorrow."

"Okay, Left. You be easy."

"Till I die, Black. Till I die." Left walked out of the door.

"Here, baby. Here are the diapers," said Black.

"Baby, will you do me one more favor? Would you get me two towels out of the bathroom? And bring me that baby powder off the dresser."

"Anything for you, precious. Where are the boys?"

She said, "I sent them to bed about two hours ago." Black returned to the room with the towels and baby powder. "Thank you, baby."

"You're welcome, precious. I am going to take a bath and go to bed. By the way, I pulled Marcus's old baby pen out of the closet so you can put Truce in it."

"All right, baby. I will be in there just as soon as I put a diaper on Truce." Shortly after Pam put a diaper on Truce, Truce fell asleep. Pam carried Truce into the bedroom and gently tucked her into the crib. Then she lay down and went right to sleep.

At about five thirty in the morning, Black was awakened by the sound of Truce crying. "Damn, what time is it?" he said to himself. "Hold up, baby. Daddy is coming."

"Don't worry about it, honey. I'll get her."

"Pam, how long have you been up?"

"Since five o'clock, for about forty minutes. She has peed on herself. I'm going to change her."

"Baby, before you go, what's for breakfast?"

"Eggs, bacon, biscuits, and rice with some red-eyed gravy."

"Shit! Baby, you must wanna make love or something."

"Ha! Boy, you're crazy."

Black got up and went to the bathroom to groom himself. After that, he headed straight to the kitchen. He received a warm welcome from his two sons, Marcus and Maurice.

"What's up, Dad?"

"Yeah, Dad, what's up?"

"Nothing but the struggle. So what's up with you-all?"

"Well, Dad," said Marcus, "today is story day at school, and it is my turn to tell a story. I am going to tell the class a story about your life in the struggle."

"First of all, son, let's get one thing straight. The struggle is not a story. A story is an account of real or imaginary events. A story is a compilation of fairy tales, myths, and legends. It's kind of like mixing the truth with falsehood. Stories are what white people tell ignorant black people. The struggle is not a story but a reality of a condition that black people go through every day in the ghetto."

"I'm sorry, Dad," said Marcus.

"No, son, you haven't done anything wrong. As a matter of fact, I am very proud of you, Marcus, because you understand and appreciate your father's contribution to the uplifting of black people regardless of the method that I use. That really means a lot to me, son. Marcus?"

"Yes, Dad?"

"I want you to go to school, and I want you to represent the struggle to the best of your ability. All right, son?"

"All right, Dad."

"So, Maurice, what are you doing at school?"

"Dad, you know me. I'm representing to the fullest."

"Keep it alive, son."

"Until the world blows up, Dad," said Maurice while demonstrating his belief, his hood, and his affiliation with his hands.

Pam entered and said, "Boy, what the hell I told you about throwing those damn gang signs?"

"Mama, I'm not in no gang. I'm in an organization."

"You ain't in shit!"

Black said, "Pam, baby, give Maurice a chance."

"I don't want my baby to get hurt or even killed because he throws the wrong gang sign or wears his hat to the wrong side."

A car horn honked outside. Pam looked out of the window. "It's Big Mama," she said. "She's going to take me to the clinic."

"Big Mama, Big Mama!" shouted Marcus and Maurice as they raced to the door to meet her.

Pam went to the bedroom to get Truce. A few minutes later, Pam returned with Truce in her arms.

Big Mama was Black's mother. She was a very beautiful, dark-skinned, full-figured woman with a medium-sized afro. She was full of wisdom and brought laughter and joy to everyone. Also, Big Mama was a member of the Black Panther Party in Chicago.

Black walked out of the door with Pam. "What's up, black woman?" he said to Big Mama as he walked over to the car and kissed her on the forehead."

"Nothing but the rent," responded Big Mama.

Black walked around to the passenger side of the car, stuck his head in the window, and kissed Truce on the side of the jaw. Then he gave Pam a short but intimate kiss.

"Marcus and Maurice!" Big Mama said. "Y'all cover up your ears and go back in the house."

"Big Mama, can we come over to your and Granddaddy's house this weekend?" Marcus asked.

"Yes, if it's all right with your mama."

"Can we, Mama? Can we go over to Big Mama's house?"

"Yes, you can go. Now, do what Big Mama told you to do."

They said, "All right. Bye, Big Mama. Bye, Mama. Bye, little sister who we've never met before."

Upon Maurice's remarks, as he and his brother walked back toward the apartment complex, everyone laughed.

"I don't know what I'm going to do with that boy," said Pam.

"He's a natural comedian," said Big Mama.

"He gets it from his grandmother," said Black.

"Baby, don't be talking about Pam's mother—she's not here to defend herself."

"I'm talking about my mother," said Black as he headed toward the apartment. Upon Black's remark, Big Mama and Pam laughed; even little Truce had a smile on her face. One would think that Truce understood every word being said.

CHAPTER 3

Shortly after the bus picked up Marcus and Maurice for school, there was a knock at the door. Black opened up the door, and it was Dirty Left. "What's up, gangster?" Black said.

Left greeted Black with the secret handshake. "Nothing. Are you here alone?"

"Yes. What's on your mind, brother?"

"Black, you wouldn't believe it, but a little bird gave me some good information. I know how to get up close to the don of the Jewish Mafia."

"Talk to me, Left. I'm listening, brother."

"Well, the little bird who whispered in my ear, who happens to be an old friend of my old man's, told me that at Don Renfro's restaurant there is an underground ring where the shot callers bet big money on full-contact fighting."

"How are we going to get in?"

"I'm glad that you asked, Black. The little bird has scheduled me for the main event fight. Me against the Jewish Mafia's best fighter, who happens to be the champion. The winner gets a hundred and fifty thousand dollars; the loser gets twenty thousand. But it costs ten grand for a nonmember to compete."

"Man, what about your knee, Left?"

"Don't worry about my knee; it's ready to go."

"Are you sure, brother?"

"Yeah, Black. It's as ready as it will ever be."

"Well, Left, you know that the money ain't no problem."

"Everything's already taken care of; I already paid for my admittance."

"Well, Left, I need you to ride with me for a minute," said Black. "Let's go."

Shortly after they got on the road, Black said to Left, "I'm going over here to round up some of those true blue soldiers for tomorrow night. We've got to make sure everything goes straight."

As they pulled up to the housing projects on the South Side they were greeted by some more of their brothers who were holding down the corner. "What's up, gangsters?" said Black.

"Nothing but the struggle," responded the men.

Black and Left got out of the car and were welcomed with the traditional handshake and hugs.

"Where's Point Blank and Hot Shot at?"

"They are in the house," said one of the brothers.

"Bet it up," said Left as he and Black headed toward the apartment.

They reached the door, and Black knocked.

"Who is it?" said a voice from the other side of the door.

"The world nigger," answered Left.

The door immediately opened. "What's up, gangster?"

Black and Dirty Left entered the room. "Where's Point Blank?"

"Here I am, gangster." Point Blank was in the corner with a sister sitting in his lap and wearing a bandana. Point Blank met Black and Left approaching him.

"Let me have a word with you," said Black. The three walked to a room.

Point Blank said, "What's up, Black?"

"I'm going to need you tomorrow night. You and about six more soldiers who ain't afraid to die!"

"Why? What's up, gangster?" Point Blank asked with concern.

"Left and I got a meeting with the white Jewish Mafia. Left has been scheduled for a big fight with the champion of full-contact fighting—a hundred grand for the winner, and I'm taking a hundred grand along with me to side bet with. Point Blank, I need you to make sure everything goes straight."

"You are calling the shots, Black. I'm with you and Left until the end."

Black and Left shook Point Blank's hand. "We will meet you tomorrow night in front of Don Renfro's restaurant at seven o'clock. Make sure that y'all come dressed to kill!" said Black as he and Left exited the room and headed toward the door.

"That's the only way that I dress," said Point Blank.

CHAPTER 4

The next day, Black was awakened by Pam. "Wake up, honey. It's time for breakfast," she said with Truce in her arms.

"Hey, ladies," Black said as his vision cleared up.

"Honey, you need to wash your face and please brush your teeth. The children and I are waiting for you at the table."

Black got up with a skip and a hop, and after he paid the bathroom a visit, he headed straight to the kitchen, where he was welcomed by the rest of the family.

"Good morning, Dad," said Marcus and Maurice.

"Good morning, brothers," Black said. "Hey, Truce, baby. I see that you have your own chair."

Pam said, "Big Mama and I went to the store, and she bought the baby chair for Truce after we left the clinic."

"So, Pam, how's Truce?"

"The doctor said that she's in better health than all of us."

"That's good," said Black. "Tomorrow we are going downtown to hear the minister of the Nation of Islam speak, and Saturday we're going to the picture shop and take a family picture."

The school bus honked the horn outside.

"Marcus, the school bus is blowing outside."

"Yes, ma'am." Marcus and Maurice gave their mother, father, and Truce kisses before they headed for the door.

Pam said, "I have to hurry up and get to work. Can you look after Truce until Big Mama comes over here and gets her?"

"Yeah, Pam. I need to spend a little time alone with my daughter."

"All right, baby. I will see you when I get in tonight," Pam said before she kissed Black and Truce and walked out of the door.

Shortly after Pam left, there was a knock at the door. Black walked to the door with Truce in one arm. It was Left.

"What's up, Left?" said Black.

"Nothing but the struggle," responded Left with excitement.

"Brother what have you been doing? You look pumped up!"

"Black, I have been punching the bag and running a few laps. I feel good, Black. I feel good! So I see that you are doing a little babysitting," said Left as he sat on the couch.

"Yeah, man. Big Mama should be here any minute to pick up Truce."

There was a knock at the door. Black walked over to the door and opened it. It was Pimp.

"Pimp, what brings you down here?"

"I came over here to see Truce. Can I hold her?"

Black handed Truce to Pimp.

"It has been almost three months since I last saw her. When can she come over and spend a weekend with me and Mechell?"

"It will have to be next week, Pimp."

"That's cool, Black. I just want her to spend a little time with the rest of the family."

There was another knock at the door. "It must be Big Mama," Black said as he walked over to open the door. "Hey, woman, what's up?" Black hugged her as she walked through the door.

"Boy, move out of the way. I know that I look good, but I'm your mama."

Upon hearing Big Mama's remark, Left and Pimp started laughing.

"Where's my grandbaby?"

"Here she is," answered Pimp while handing Truce to her.

She grabbed Truce and headed out the door. "You boys be good!"

Black said, "Pimp, I got a deal—or should I say, I got a plan to make some serious grand."

"Shit, brother, make me understand," responded Pimp.

"You know the cat who got the chain of restaurants and corner stores, and also all of the heroin?"

"Yeah, Black, I know who you are talking about," said Pimp. "You're talking about that cat Don Renfro."

"Left and I are going to fade him tonight."

"Shit, my brother. I'm with you," Pimp said with sincerity. "I can get my soldiers, and we can blow that punk off the map!"

"Hold up, Pimp. It's not time for that. Besides, that's unprofessional. That chump has got the mayor, governor, chief of police, judges, and the city council on the payroll, so keep that in mind. Tonight, Left has a championship fight against the Mafia's full-contact fighting champ. I'm taking a hundred grand with me to side bet. You know that the Mafia's going to be betting ten-to-one odds."

"In that case," Pimp said, "that dude has got to be a bad motherfucker! Dirty Left, are you ready?"

Left responded with a smile.

"The boy is ready," said Black.

"So what time are we going?" asked Pimp.

"You and a couple of your boys meet me in front of Don Renfro's restaurant at eleven o'clock tonight, and be dressed to kill. If they tremble, we are going to close the motherfucker down!"

"Aye, Black. I'm going to step, but before I go ..." Pimp pulled a large roll of money out of his pocket. "Here's two grand for Truce."

"Okay, bro," said Black while putting the money in his pocket.

"Also, I need you to walk me outside. You boys took my gun out front."

"Come on. Left and I will walk you out there. You know how those young soldiers are."

"Yeah, Black, I understand."

Five hours passed by very quickly. It was now time for Black and Left to take the opportunity that they had been looking for. They'd face the powers that be only minutes from now. Black had taken a good shower and put on his black snakeskin loafers, blue three-piece suit with black pinstripes, black shades, a black hat, and a black cane with a smoke-black mink coat. There were only two things missing, and those were his two smoking demons: two chrome Colt .45s with pearl handles on them.

There was a knock at the door, and Black opened it. There were two soldiers in front of his door, in black mechanic suits. "Gangster Black, we are here to escort you to the spot."

"Oh, yeah?" said Black. "Then what's the password?"

"One love, nigger," responded the two in unison.

Black already knew that they were on his side. Besides, how in the hell could they have gotten past the trigger-happy security team out front? On the other hand, people weren't allowed to come in the neighborhood after eight o'clock unless they lived here or were close relatives of Black because Black had established a curfew that his soldiers enforced. This was done to ensure the safety of the children.

"What are we waiting on?" said Black after grabbing his black briefcase.

"It's on you, Gangster Black. You are calling the shots."

"Shit! Let's go," said Black with excitement.

When they made it to the parking lot, there were three cars lined up. Two were twin black Eldorados, both 1968 model convertibles. Point Blank was sitting in back of one, and Hot Shot was in the other. Point Blank leaned his head out the window and said, "Gangster Black, let's do this!" Black threw his hand up and gave Point Blank a serious smile. The third car was a cocaine white

Lincoln Continental with gangster whitewall tires. The soldiers who were with Black said, "This is your ride," as one of them opened the door for him to get in.

When Black got inside of the car, he was greeted by his right-hand man, Left. "What's up, Gangster Black?"

"What's up, gangster?" answered Black. "Are you ready, Left?"

"As ready as I will ever be." Left had on some black silk baggy pants, a black silk vest with no shirt on under it, black shades, black snakeskin loafers, and black gloves. His hair was pinned up in a ponytail. He was a six foot eleven, 310-pound albino dressed up like a stripper.

When they made it to the spot, they were greeted by Pimp and a couple of soldiers. Point Blank opened the door for Black and Left to get out. Black got out with his briefcase in his hand, and Left got out behind him. Pimp greeted them both with a big smile.

"Damn, Pimp," said Left. "You are as sharp as a tack!"

"Shit, look at nigger Black," said Pimp. "Black, brother, you've got to be the cleanest mother in the state."

"Shit, Pimp, I just try to do my best. Besides, they don't call me Black the Mack for nothing."

"What's the holdup?" said Left with a sly grin on his face. "I'm ready to show my ass."

"Now, that's what I'm talking about," Pimp said. "Let's kick some ass!"

The street in front of the restaurant was filled with all kinds of big shots jumping out of Rolls-Royces and Cadillacs. Black and the crew entered the doors of the restaurant. Left stepped to one of the waiters and whispered in his ear, "We are here for full-contact fighting. I'm scheduled to fight in the main event against the champ."

The waiter told Left to follow him, and Left signaled to the rest of the crew. Black, Pimp, Point Blank, Hot Shot, and the other men followed Left and the waiter behind the bar, through a door into the kitchen, through the back door, and into a big parking lot.

Black was suspicious, so he put his hand on one of the Colts hidden under his mink coat. He said to the waiter, "Where the fuck are we going?"

"Don't worry," said the waiter as they approached a door that had "Stairs" written above it. The waiter then knocked on the door, the door opened, and there was an old black man who stood in the door with a pipe in his mouth.

Upon seeing Left, the old man's face lit up like a streetlight. "What's up, boy?" he said to Left. Then he said to the waiter while handing him a twenty-dollar bill, "It's okay, Bobby. I've got them."

The waiter took the money from the old man in the doorway and walked away. He took one last look at Left and said, "Didn't you say you were going to fight the champ?" Left nodded. "I wish you luck—you're going to need it. That guy is a killer. He has killed everyone that he's fought." Then the waiter walked away.

Before he got out of sight, Left called across the parking lot, "Bobby! Bobby!" The waiter stopped and turned around. Left said to him, "When I beat the champ, you can come and work for me." Upon hearing this, everyone laughed even the old man.

Then the old man said, "Come on in. Y'all, the first fight is about to begin."

Left and the crew entered the room, which was filled with cigar smoke and was probably big enough to land an airplane in it. The first thing that caught their eyes in the room besides the large ring was the sight of Don Renfro sitting at a table with three woman and his bodyguards. The sight of Don Renfro made everyone with Left feel their flesh crawl because they would like nothing more than to kill Don Renfro.

The old black man told Left and the crew to hold up. Then he went across the room and whispered in a guy's ear who seemed to be watching everything. The guy signaled to another black guy, who came over. After a few words passed between the three, the old man returned with the other black man.

Black said, "Look at this weak-ass nigger, sell out motherfucker. I should've killed your ass a long time ago," said Black with fire in his voice.

"Y'all cool out," said the old man as he stepped between Black, Left, and the other guy. "I just came to show you losers to your table. And just in case you want to bet something, Don Renfro is taking all bets with ten-to-one odds."

"Tell your man that we've got a hundred and fifty thousand grand," said Black.

"Make it two hundred grand," said Pimp. "I've got fifty grand on my nigga Left."

"Damn, y'all losers are donating a lot of money. Well, it doesn't matter," said the guy who offered to show Black to their table. "Y'all will be going home one short. The champ is going to kill Left!"

Upon hearing this, Left laughed and said, "It's so sad when your own people go against you, especially when you are standing up for the community. But just like all sellouts and niggers, brother, you will go down."

"Come on, Left," said Black as they walked to the table chosen for them. Upon sitting at the table, Black said to Left, "Brother, it's on us. The chance to change the condition of black people in the ghettos of Chicago is in our hands. Left, we can make a fashion statement so strong that the powers that be will have to respect our demands."

"Black, you are so right," replied Left. "Tonight when I fight, I fight not only for integrity of the disciples, vice lords, black Stone Rangers, Mickey Cobras, high supreme gangsters, and Black Panthers, but for all blacks, Latinos, Hispanics, Chinese, and every deprived and minority child in the world. If it be the will of God, I won't lose."

Their conversation was interrupted by a very tall white guy. "Excuse me," said the guy to Black.

Black answered, "Yeah?"

The man said, "Don wants to speak with you."

Black stood up and walked over to the table where Don Renfro was, but not without Left by his side. When they made it to Don Renfro's table, it seemed to be heavily guarded by bodyguards. But as soon as Don Renfro laid eyes on Black and Left, he clapped his hands and ordered the women to leave him.

"Have a seat, boys," said Don Renfro.

Neither Black nor Left moved. At that time, one of the don's bodyguards said to them, "The boss said have a seat."

Black replied, "He wasn't talking to us."

Don Renfro asked, "What's the matter, fellas?"

Black answered, "You said, 'Boys, have a seat.' Boys don't come in places like this."

"I'm sorry," said Don Renfro. "Excuse me. Would you please have a seat with me?"

Upon hearing this, Black and Left sat at the table with Don Renfro.

"So I hear that you men have some wages that you wanna put up," Don Renfro said.

"Well, it depends on the odds that you're willing to put up," Black replied.

"I give everybody ten-to-one odds."

"In that case, we've got two hundred grand," Black said as he put his suitcase on the table and opened it.

Upon seeing this, Don Renfro clapped his hands, and immediately a guy came over to the table. Don Renfro told the guy to bring him two million. Shortly after the men left, he returned with two suitcases, one in each hand, and placed them on the table. Don Renfro ordered the men to open them. The guy opened the suitcases, and both of them appeared to be filled with hundred-dollar bills.

Black said, "It's a bet then." He and Left returned to the table with Pimp and the rest of the crew.

Pimp said, "Is everything straight?"

Black answered, "Yeah, everything's straight. He just showed us two million. There's only one thing left."

"What's that?" asked Pimp.

"For Left to put the so-called champ in the dust," answered Black.

"Let's get the show on the road!" yelled the man in the ring. "The first fight is on the way."

The first fight went by fast, and so did the second one. Then it was time for Left and the big fight. The whole community was betting on it. The commentator announced, "The man in this corner, fighting out of the toughest ghettos in Chicago: Dirty Left! Over in this corner, fighting in all kinds of tough contests the world over, the undisputed, undefeated champ of full-contact fighting: Animal!"

After that, a big white guy came out with a black headband. Shortly after the bell rang, Left and the Champ faced off.

The champ came with a kick to Left's side, to his face. The large audience roared. The champ started bouncing around the ring like a martial arts master. Left rushed the champ and ran head-on into a right jab, followed by a punch to the solar plexus, which caused Left to bend over and meet the champ's knee in his face. That busted Left's lip and nose, sending Left to the floor. Black shouted from the table.

Left got up from the floor and began to lick his thumbs and flick his left jab while he scooted closer to the champ, still flicking his left jab with his hand open. The champ swung at Left but was unsuccessful in connecting with Left. Left kept his routine up, flicking his left jab in the face of the champ without touching him. As Left's arm begin to stretch over the head of the champ, Left released his right, which exploded in the face of the champ, busting his nose and cutting him under the eye at the same time. That lick sent the champ to the floor. Black and Pimp screamed at the table.

Left screamed at the champ, "Get up! Get up!"

The champ got up very slowly and then rushed Left. The champ faked as if he was going to kick Left, and he swung an overhand right. Left sidestepped him and caught him around the neck with a choke hold. The champ began to wave his arms in the air. After about a minute, one could see the champ's knees buckling.

Left then released the choke hold on the champ, grabbed him around the waist, and picked him up in the air over his head. Left turned around and faced Black at the table. Black shouted, "Drive it home, my nigga!" Left slammed the champ on his head as hard as he could. This knocked the champ out and left him shaking as if he was having a seizure.

The referee stepped in, stopped the fight, and signaled for someone to bring the stretcher. Two guys immediately entered the ring with a stretcher and hauled away Left's opponent. Meanwhile, the referee announced that Left was the winner of the match and was the new international heavyweight, full-contact fighting champion. The referee gave Left the championship belt. By that time, Black, Pimp, and the others at the table made their way to the ring.

Don Renfro sat at his table with a puzzled look on his face. He couldn't believe that he had just lost $2 million to a local street gang. As Left and Black made their way out of the ring, Don Renfro and two guys were waiting on them with three suitcases in their hands. One of the guys handed Left a suitcase, and the other guy handed two suitcases to Black. By that time, Point Blank had sent one of the soldiers outside to tell the other soldiers to be on standby just in case the Mafia tried to ambush Black and the crew when they came out.

After Black was handed the two suitcases, Don Renfro said to Black and Left, "You guys won fair and square, but if you wanna make some real money, I have a spot for the both of you. We will be traveling all over the world. You guys will be making at least a million every fight. So what do you say?"

"It sounds nice," said Left, "but we are fighting for the liberation of our people, and you can't pay us enough money to sell our people out if you lived for a thousand years. Each and every one of their lives is precious and priceless."

"We are out of here," Black said.

Don Renfro's boys made a break by pulling out their guns, but Point Blank and Pimp had the jump on them and pulled out sawed-off shotguns. Black pulled out both of his pearl-handled, nickel-plated .45s.

Don Renfro said to his boys, "Put your damn guns up!" Then he said to Black, "Excuse my boys for the interruption."

Black responded, "Shit, it don't even matter. We can do the shit up in here like the Wild West!"

"That won't be necessary," Don Renfro replied.

"Well, we're outta here," said Black as he and the crew disappeared through the door. Waiting for them outside were a few of Black's soldiers. They had the cocaine-white Lincoln in front of the entrance with the suicide doors let up, and the soldiers were standing in front, beside, and behind the Lincoln with their guns out. Across the street were soldiers lying on the hood, standing in front and behind them with guns pointed at the entrance of the restaurant. Black, Pimp, and Left got in the Lincoln as Point Blank let the door down and got in on the passenger side. The driver pulled away from the scene with the rest of the crew behind them.

Black, Left, and Pimp celebrated their win over Don Renfro in the back of the car. "We did it! Where are we headed?" asked Pimp.

"How about Suzy's?" Black said.

"That's cool."

The driver took them to Ms. Suzy's store, and they found the closed sign on the door. "Damn," said Black. "Suzy's is closed, but her Cadillac is still here, so she's still here."

"Man, I hate to hear her damn mouth! She's going to be talking shit."

"I know somebody who can get us in with no problem," said Black with a smile on his face. He looked at Left. "Come on, brother. You know that Suzy's crazy about you."

"All right, man," said Left as Point Blank opened the door for him. Left slowly walked up to the door and gently knocked on it.

Suzy came to the door with intentions of cursing someone out for disregarding her closed sign, but when she saw Left, she forgot all about cursing. "Hey, baby," she said as she opened the door and hugged Left. "What happened to your lip?"

"It's a long story," said Left.

"Come on in, honey. Ain't nobody here but me. Let me take care of that lip for you."

Left grabbed Suzy by the hand, looked her in the eyes, and said, "I need you to do a favor for me."

"What is it? You know that I will do anything for you, Left."

"Well, Suzy, we need to use your room in the back. Black and I will pay you."

"Baby, you don't have to pay me anything."

"Thanks," said Left as he kissed Suzy on the cheek. Suzy's face lit up like a streetlight. Left waved his hand for Pimp and Black to get out of the car. Black and Pimp walked up to the door. Black then knocked on the door.

Suzy shouted, "Boy, bring your ass in here!" Black and Pimp walked in. Suzy had a bottle of rubbing alcohol with some tissue, and she was rubbing alcohol on a cut under Left's right eye. Black stopped and stared at Suzy with a big smile on his face. "What the hell are you looking at?" Suzy asked Black.

"Can we use the back room?"

"You know where it is."

"Damn, Suzy. You don't have to go off on me," Black joked. He led Pimp to the room with two suitcases in his hands. "Left, we need you in here."

Left got up, and Suzy said to him, "Damn, that's how it is."

"No," said Left. "We've got to handle some business."

Left walked in. Black and Pimp were sitting at a table with the suitcases on the table. "Grab a seat so that we can count this cheese," said Black. "Put them in stacks of fifty grand." He opened up both suitcases.

After a few hours, they finished counting the money. Black said, "It's all here." He counted out $500,000 and gave it to Pimp. Then he counted out $500,000 and gave it to Left.

Left refused to take it. "Put it up in the family treasure. I have a hundred and fifty thousand to work with. If I need it, I will holler at you."

"Well, Left, you already know that if you need it, you know where it is."

"True that," responded Left.

"I'm going to break Suzy off a few grand," Black said.

"Me too," said Pimp as he counted out $5,000.

"I'm going to give her five thousand too," said Left.

"That means that she will have fifteen thousand dollars. Suzy!"

"Black, what the hell do you want?" answered Suzy as she came into the room.

"Here," said Black. "This is fifteen thousand dollars that we are giving you."

"I'm not giving y'all shit in return!" snapped Suzy. Everyone laughed at Suzy's remarks, even Suzy.

"Well, brothers," said Black, "are y'all ready to get up outta here?"

"Yeah," said Pimp. "I've got to get back home to my queen and children."

Left said, "I need a hot bath. I can feel myself becoming stiff and sore."

"You can take a shower over my house," replied Suzy.

"Nah, precious. I need to go home and get some rest. I have a big day ahead of me. Maybe some other time."

"Okay, I understand."

Black, Pimp, and Left headed for the door. Before Left walked out of the door, he turned around and gave Suzy a kiss on the cheek. She smiled and said, "What was that for?"

"I will tell you one day," responded Left as he walked out the door.

After they dropped off Pimp and made it to Black's apartment, Black said to Left, "Brother, you might as well spend the night over here because I know that you're too tired to go home."

"No, Black. Thanks, but I need to go home." He got out of the car, walked to his own, and slowly pulled away.

Black said to himself, "They don't come no realer than that."

On Left's way home, he drove about five miles faster than the normal speed limit and was pulled over by the police. The police turned on the siren. Left looked through his rearview mirror and saw the light flashing on top of the police car. "Damn," he said to himself as he pulled over. Left watched through the rearview mirror as the door opened on the police car. He hoped it wasn't one of those racist white police who got off on harassing young black males, or one of those black police officers who made his living by trying to prove his loyalty to his fellow white officers by showing off on young black males in front of them.

"Excuse me, sir," said the officer. "May I see your driver's license." The officer wasn't white. The officer was a black woman.

"Yes, ma'am," answered Left as he handed his driver's license to her. *Man, she's beautiful,* he thought to himself.

"Sir, you were going twenty in a fifteen mile-per-hour lane. I'm going to have to write you a ticket."

"Yes, ma'am," said Left. "You are exactly right. I have no problem with you writing me a ticket—just as long as you let me take you out."

"You don't even know me," said the policewoman. "What are you trying to do, bribe me? I could arrest you right now if I wanted to. I don't even know you. You are a stranger."

Left put a real serious look on his face and said, "I don't know you either. You are also a stranger, but in life we take chances every day. I took a chance stopping in this dark alley when you signaled for me to stop. You could have been one of those white cops who love to harass young black men, or one of those black officers who love to show off in front of white cops."

"But I'm not," interrupted the policewoman.

"Please let me finish, ma'am, if that's all right with you?"

"Yes, you can finish."

"The point is I don't know who you are, but I still took a chance pulling over. On the other hand, you took a chance when you pulled me over in this dark alley all by yourself. I could be a lunatic or one of those people who would love to catch a police officer in a dark alley."

"But you are not," she interrupted.

"How do you know, sister? I'm a stranger."

"I just know it."

"Naw, sister, you don't know me. Just like I don't know you. But the point is we both took a chance. All I'm asking you to do is to take a chance to allow us the opportunity to become a little more acquainted with each other, but I'm sorry if I offended you. Besides, that's probably against your policy to talk to a man from your own race."

"Excuse me, brother. It seems to me that you have a problem with police officers."

"No, sister, I don't have a problem with police officers. I have a problem with crooked police officers."

Left's strong conversation made her forget all about why she had pulled him over in the first place. She was so mesmerized by Left that she decided to give him her address. "Here's my name and address. What time are you coming to pick me up?"

"About eleven o'clock," answered Left as she began to walk back to the police car. "Excuse me, Maria," said Left. "You forgot something. Didn't you?"

"Oh," said Maria. "I forgot to give you your ticket." She handed Left the ticket that she had written him for speeding.

"Do you want me to follow you to make sure you make it up out of here safely?" asked Left.

"Naw, brother," answered Maria. "I'm a big girl, and I'm from the hood."

Left watched as Maria disappeared into the night. Left thought to himself, *Okay, God. Let her be the right one.* He drove away.

CHAPTER 5

Black was awakened the next morning by the smell of Pam's cooking. He got up with a smile on his face as he went to the bathroom to brush his teeth. After Black finished, he headed straight for the kitchen and was greeted as usual.

Black said to Pam, "Honey, you know that we are going to the Unity rally to hear the minister of the Nation of Islam speak at twelve o'clock."

"Yes," answered Pam.

There was a knock at the door, and Black got up and answered the door. It was Left all dressed up with a big smile on his face. "What's up, champ?" said Black. "You've got a big smile on your face."

"Oh, brother, let me tell you."

"But before you tell me, come on in here and have some breakfast with us."

"Thanks, bro, but I've already eaten. I'm in a little rush. I met this foxy sister last night, and I'm headed right over to pick her up. I will meet y'all at the church. Tell everybody that I said what's up. I'm out of here." They did the sacred handshake.

Black walked back into the kitchen with a grin on his face.

"What's up, baby? Who was that at the door?" asked Pam.

"Baby, that was Left."

"Did he want some breakfast?"

"No, Pam. He said that he's already eaten."

"Okay, so why are you smiling?"

"Because Left has finally met someone, and he seems really interested in her."

"Who is she?"

"I don't know—Left did not even mention her name."

"Well, that's good," said Pam. "Just as long as he's happy."

"Left said to tell everyone hi, and he will meet us at the church. Baby, that was a good breakfast, just like the rest of your delicious meals." He got up from the table and walked around to the other side of the table. He unstrapped Truce from her baby chair. "Truce and I are going in the living room to look at the news," he said.

Pam said, "Marcus, Maurice, go to your room and get ready for school."

"Yes, ma'am."

While Black watched the news, a live broadcast flashed. The reporters were live at an abandoned apartment complex about a half a mile up the street from his apartment. The reporters said that a thirty-five-year-old man, Mike Donahue, was found amputated, with his head and penis cut off. Investigators found his head in an old refrigerator in one of the apartments with his penis stuck in his mouth. Although gang graffiti was found on the wall, the investigators were trying to determine whether or not it was gang related.

"Damn," Black said to himself. "That's the dude Left fought against last night. Don Renfro must have had him knocked off after he lost a fight. I've got to talk to Left and let him know what's going on. We might have to take Don Renfro to war."

While Black sat in front of the TV with Truce in his arms, someone knocked at the door. Black opened the door, and it was his father, who was known as Big Daddy to the family and Moses to the people in the streets. Big Daddy was a freedom fighter and a civil rights activist. On many occasions, Big Daddy had gone to jail for protesting with other civil rights activists.

"What's up, son?"

"Nothing but the struggle," answered Black with surprise on his face. "Come on in, Dad. So what brings you over here this morning?"

"Son, I'm glad that you asked," answered Big Daddy while taking Truce out of Black's arms. "But I think that you already know."

"Naw, Dad. I haven't the slightest idea what you are talking about."

"Does the name Don Renfro ring a bell?"

"Yeah. What about him?"

"Word out on the street is that you and your boys took him for two million dollars."

"Dad, we beat him fair and square."

"Son, there's no such thing as fair and square with Don Renfro."

Marcus and Maurice walked in. "Hey, Granddaddy!"

"Hey, boys!"

"Granddaddy, can we come over and visit you and Grandma?"

"Yeah, if that's all right with your father."

"Hey, Dad," says Marcus, "can we go over to Granddaddy's house this weekend?"

"Yeah, you can go over to Granddaddy's house."

Big Daddy handed Truce to Black and opened the door. "Son, you have a gift and also the potential to be a good leader for our people—but you can't straddle the fence. You've got one foot in the water and the other one on dry land, with a fire burning underneath you. What are you going to do when your water breaks?" Then he walked out of the door.

This put serious thought in Black's mind. Black took Truce into the bedroom so that Pam could dress her.

Shortly after, the school bus began to blow outside. "Marcus, Maurice, the school bus is outside," Black said.

"Okay, Dad," they answered as they raced outside.

Pam entered the room with Truce in her arms, and waited patiently for Black to finish dressing. Upon Black entering the room, he was greeted with a warm smile from Pam.

"Hey, ladies," he said with a smile on his face. "Are you ready to go?"

"Yeah, baby," said Pam. "We are waiting on you."

"Let's go," said Black as he walked toward the door. "Ladies first."

Pam walked through the door with Truce in her arms.

Shortly after they make it to the coliseum, Black, Pam, and Truce made their way inside and sat down.

Before the minister spoke, Left looked behind and spotted Pam and Black sitting in the middle row with two chairs next to them that were vacant. Left said to Maria, "Come on, precious. Let's go sit with my brother and his wife. I want you to meet them."

Left and Maria made it to the row where Black and Pam were sitting, and Pam spotted them. "Hey! Honey, there's Left. And that must be the new woman that he met."

Left said, "Black, Pam, what's up?"

"Hey, Left," said Pam as Left and Maria sat down next to them.

"Pam and Black, this is Maria. Maria, this is my brother Black and his wife, Pam. And this is their beautiful daughter, who happens to be my goddaughter, Truce."

"Pleased to meet you," said Maria as she extended her hand to shake both Black and Pam's hands.

"Please to meet you too," said Pam.

"You have a very cute little girl," said Maria. "Can I hold her?"

"Sure." Pam stood up to hand Truce over to Maria. Maria gently took Truce out of Pam's arms.

Soon the MC announced the minister of the Nation of Islam. The crowd was immediately captivated by the minister's opening. He spoke on the importance of accepting one's own and being oneself. The minister spoke for about an hour and a half, but he got his message across so clear that Black and Left were convinced their next step would definitely be Islam.

CHAPTER 6

The months passed by. After a year, both sides of Truce's family grew very attached to her. Left and Maria became even closer—so close that Left decided to propose to her.

"Honey," Maria said to Left, "get up, baby. I've cooked you breakfast."

As Left opened his eyes, he was greeted with a warm smile by the woman he had searched for and longed for his whole entire life. Maria stood there with a well dressed plate in her hand and wore nothing but her panties and Left's shirt, which fit her like a gown.

"Baby, what time is it?"

"It's nine o'clock," answered Maria as she sat on the side of the bed.

Left sat up. "Baby, what did I do to deserve this?"

Maria gave a sly, sexy smile before saying, "What we did last night meant nothing to you?"

"No, honey, I didn't mean it like that."

"I know, baby. Let me feed you."

After Maria finished feeding Left, he expressed his feelings to Maria. "Baby, you make me feel like a black king."

"Thank you, honey! You make me feel like a black queen. Well, I have to take a bath and get ready for work. I don't want the chief to come down on me."

"Do you want me to have a word with him?"

"No, baby. If they found out my boyfriend is a black gangster disciple, they would probably turn my name over to the FBI."

"To be honest with you, Maria, the FBI is probably already investigating us."

"Honey, you've got to be kidding."

"No, I'm not kidding. Whenever black people unify to bring about a change for themselves without allowing the government to put its nose in it, the FBI considers them a threat to the American way."

Maybe Left was a psychic, but sure enough, there was a white van outside in the parking lot of the apartment complex. It appeared to be a phone company van, but inside were two guys with headphones on, and they could clearly hear Left and Maria's conversation. When Maria left to go to work, the white van followed her from a long distance.

Meanwhile, after Left showered, he went over to Black's house to let him know about his plans of marrying Maria. As Left pulled into the apartment complex, he was greeted by some of the young brothers who looked up to him. Left paid his respects by throwing his hand in the air. After Left parked his car, he knocked on the door.

Black opened the door. "What's up, gangster? How's the struggle?"

"Black, brother, I can't lie: I'm enjoying it. I'm seriously thinking about proposing to Maria. What do you think about that, bro?"

"Man, I think that you should go for it. Maria is a very beautiful and successful sister, and most of all she loves you for who you are."

"Black, you are so right. I'm thinking about going to the jewelry store and picking out an engagement ring. There's nothing to it but to do it."

"Left, I will ride over to the jewelry shop."

"All right, brother. Let's go. By the way, Black, where's my goddaughter?"

"She's over at Pimp's house. She will be over there for a couple of weeks. Pimp has a little daughter the same age as Truce, so she has someone to play with."

"You know, Black, it seems as if it were yesterday when you brought her home. Now look at her. Next year, Truce will be in the first grade."

"Yeah, Left, you are exactly right. And before you know it, she will be meeting boys and dating. I don't know how in the hell that I'm going to deal with it. Well, anyway, brother, let's go pick out the ring."

When Left and Black made it to the jewelry shop, the owner of the jewelry shop was putting the closed sign in the window. Black knocked on the window. The store owner came to the door. He was a short, middle-aged white man. "We're closed. Didn't you see the sign on the door?" stated the little man, looking at Black and Left through the glass door.

"Man, open the door," said Black. "We are here to buy an engagement ring."

The little man opened the door with a frown on his face. "I'm going to let you in after closing this one time."

Black laughed at the little man as he and Left entered the jewelry shop. Left and Black headed straight to the counter to look at the engagement rings.

"So which one you want?" asked the little man.

"Let me see that one with that nice-sized diamond on it." The clerk handed Left the ring from behind the counter. "What you think about this one, Black?"

"Now, this one is sharp, brother."

"Sir, I will take this one."

The man said, "Son, are you sure? It's pretty expensive. I have another one that's a lot less than this one."

"No, sir. I want this one. I don't care what it costs."

"Well, it costs thirty-five hundred dollars."

Left pulled a large roll of money out of his pocket and counted thirty-five hundred-dollar bills, putting them on the counter. The man put the ring inside of a little box. He put the ring on the counter as he took the money off the counter. "You have a nice day," said the little man as Left and Black walked out of the door.

"Left, I need for you to take me back home. I have to go pick up Pam from work. You know that they changed her work hours at the nursing home."

"Okay, bro," Left said as they got into the car. Shortly after that, they made it to Black's house.

"Left, why don't you come on in and chill for a little while with me?"

"Shit ain't no problem."

After Black and Left went inside, Black said, "Would you care for a beer?"

"No, man. Maria be tripping in shit when I be drinking and driving."

"Left, Maria is keeping you in line, isn't she?"

"Yeah, bro. She's something else."

"Have you met Maria's family?"

"Yeah. They live in DC. Maria's mother is very beautiful, and her father is as cool as a fan in the winter."

"So I see that you've got everything pretty much together. Well, Left, Pam and I checked out some houses in the suburbs, and we picked out one that we liked. It costs a little bit over seventy-five thousand dollars, so I decided to go ahead and get it now that we can afford it. It's a two-story, five-bedroom, with a two-door garage. There's a basketball hoop and swimming pool in the backyard."

"Okay, Black. You and Pam are stepping up in life."

"Left, it's time for all black people to step up in life. Brother, our ancestors were kings and queens in Africa, but this system in America has degenerated us into animals and beast-like things. One day we shall overcome."

"True that, brother. True that," responded Left as he shook hands with Black. "Well, I need to get back home."

"Okay, Left. Go ahead and pop the question to Maria."

"Yeah, true that. I'm out of here, Black. Until I die, brother." Left walked out the front door.

CHAPTER 7

Left proposed to Maria, and she said yes. They planned the wedding for the first of June. Maria's parents came in from DC. Meanwhile, Black bought Left and Maria a house as a wedding gift, and a few more elite disciples bought Left a black Cadillac.

It was the last day of May, and the big day was tomorrow. Maria and her mother were staying at Black's house with Pam and Truce. Black, Marcus, and Maurice were staying over at Left and Maria's place with Left's and Maria's fathers. The three of them played dominos and sipped on wine coolers that they had poured in cups while Marcus and Maurice sat in front of the TV as they ate.

The telephone rang, and Maria's father picked up the phone. "Hello? Hey, baby. How's your mother? Okay, he's playing dominos." He put the phone down and called out, "Leroy?"

"Yes, sir?" answered Left. Leroy was Left's real name.

"Maria's on the phone, and she wants to talk to you."

Left took the phone. "Hello, baby. Yeah, I love you too." Left took the phone in the other room. "Baby, tomorrow we are going to be Mr. and Mrs. Leroy Jackson. Yeah, I know. Maria, please don't start crying. Yeah, honey, I know. Okay, baby, I will see you tomorrow. I love you too. Bye."

After Left hung up the phone, he walked back into the kitchen. "Hey, I'm going to take a bath and go to bed."

"Hold up, son. We have these people coming over here for your bachelor party," said Maria's father.

"I didn't know that you were throwing me a bachelor party."

Black said, "Yeah, man. My dad is on his way over here to get Marcus and Maurice. He told me earlier today, and PB and a few more soldiers are on their way over here with some food and beer. Left, man, I wish that my brother Frank could be out for your wedding. He missed my and Pam's wedding. I know that Frank would love to see you get married."

"Yeah, I wish Frank was here. Frank used to take care of us."

"Frank taught me everything that I know—how to hustle, how to fight. Left, do you remember how Frank used to make us put the boxing gloves on and fight against him?"

"Yeah. Do you remember when he used to make us fight against cats that were bigger and older than us?"

"Yeah. Remember when he showed us how to do the three-card moley?" Left chuckled. "Yeah, Black, Frank is a true soldier."

"That Frank must be a real soldier," said Maria's father.

"Yes, sir," answered Black. "I remember when I was little, there was an old woman who had her electricity turned off and was about three months behind on rent. Frank paid the bill, and he paid her rent up for three months. He bought her some groceries and also put some money in her pocket. That old woman called Frank her son, and she loved him like one till she passed. Frank was the only family that she had. In 1986, when she departed this material world, she left everything that she had to Frank. Mother put it into storage for Frank. Well, anyway, tomorrow is your big day, Left."

A car horn blew outside. "It might be my old man, here to pick up Marcus and Maurice." Black walked over and looked through the curtain. Sure enough, it was Big Daddy. "Marcus, Maurice! Big Daddy is here to pick you up." Marcus and Maurice told their father that they loved him as they raced through the door.

Shortly after, PB and some more people arrived with beer, wine, champagne, and food. The party lasted for a couple of hours, and afterward everyone was gone except the three. Left went right to sleep. The night passed by very quickly, and soon it was time for Left to fulfill his promise that he had made unto himself when he first met Maria.

Left rose early and headed straight to the shower. Then he went into the kitchen to drink a glass of milk. He was greeted by Black and Maria's father, who was cooking breakfast.

"Son, you are just in time for breakfast," said Maria's father.

"Yeah, big G," replied Black. "You'd better put something in your stomach. You are about to jump a pretty big broom."

"No, thanks. I only want a cup of coffee."

After Black and Maria's father got themselves dressed, everyone headed over to the church. The church was located on the west side of Chicago. As they entered the church, they were met by Big Mama and Big Daddy.

"Hey, baby," Big Mama said to Left. "It's about time that you got settled down."

"Yes, ma'am," said Left as he hugged her and kissed her cheek.

"Watch out now, boy," said Big Daddy as he hugged Left. "I'm proud of you. You take good care of that girl."

"Yes, sir," said Left.

Black said to his dad, "This is Maria's father."

"Pleased to meet you," said Maria's father as he extended his hand to Big Daddy.

"It's a pleasure," said Big Daddy as he shook Maria's father's hand.

They walked inside the church. Big Baddy, Big Mama, and Maria's father sat on the front bench next to Pam, Truce, and Left's sister. Left and Black went into a room.

"Brother this is an old ending and a brand-new beginning," said Black.

"Yeah, bro. This is it. This is what I have been praying to God for: a strong black woman that I can spend my life with."

"You know what James Brown said?"

"What did he say, Gangster Black?"

"This is a man's world, but it wouldn't be nothing without a woman or a girl."

"Ha! True that. Old James Brown said something then, didn't he?"

"Yes, he did."

Someone knocked on the door. "Hey, Left, it's Big Daddy."

"Yes, sir," answered Left.

"The wedding is about to begin."

"Okay, Big Daddy. We're on our way out."

"Left, are you ready, brother? The last day to play the field."

"Yeah, I'm ready, Gangster Black. Let's step."

As they opened the door, they heard a woman playing the piano as if it was her last day. They made it into the room where everyone else was at, and Left was greeted with a room full of smiles. It also surprised Left to see three rows of benches filled up with some of his disciple brothers.

The music suddenly stopped. The woman on the piano begun to play the traditional wedding song. The people who sat on the rows of benches turned around and looked toward the back of the church. Maria was escorted down the aisle by her father. Maria lit the whole church up like the sun.

"Look at Maria," said Black.

"Man, this is it," said Left

Maria and her daughter stood next to Left and Black in front of the altar. Maria had on a powder-blue wedding gown with white shoes. Left wore a royal-blue silk suit, a black tie, and a pair of black snakeskin shoes. They looked like the perfect couple—a combination of the ghetto and the black upper middle class.

Maria's father had always felt that no man would ever be good enough for his daughter, but Maria's father noticed the way that her face lit up whenever Left was in her presence. This, along with a few things more, enabled Maria's father to let go of one of the few things that gave him a reason to exist and a reason to fight even harder for the liberation of black people and all oppressed people regardless of color. Besides, Maria's father had once been in the same position as Left. Maria's mother's parents had felt the same way about him, but look at how he had turned out. He was a former Black Stone Ranger, but look at him now: the governor of Maryland. He didn't give up on the struggle; instead, he realized that there were many more levels and degrees of the struggle that needed to be challenged, and also that there were many more significant spots that were vacant of black people that needed to be occupied. Upon realizing this, he allowed himself the opportunity to develop, grow, and evolve into something that was loved by some, hated by some, but respected by all: a black man with knowledge and a vision.

Maria's mother was a very quiet and beautiful yellow-skinned black woman from Birmingham, Alabama, who had met Maria's father in Chicago while she was attending college. Maria's mother had always dreamed of Maria marrying a doctor or a lawyer. Left was not a doctor or a lawyer, but there was no denying that he was a strong black man.

The preacher entered the sanctuary from a side door. The Reverend Ben Woods of South Side Baptist Church had known Black and Left since they were kids. As a matter of fact, the reverend and Big Daddy were a part of the civil rights movement. "Leroy," said the reverend.

"Yes, sir."

"I'm so proud of you, son. Where's your father?"

"He should be on the way here."

"If Bertha was here, she would be so proud of you."

"Yeah," said Left. "I really miss my mother, even though I really never got a chance to know her. I was only nine years old when she passed away."

"Well," said the reverend, "I see that you've got old Cory here to be your right-hand man—or should I say best man?"

Black said, "You know how we do it."

"Let's get this wedding on the road," replied Reverend Woods as he walked behind the altar. "We are gathered here today to join these two people in holy matrimony. Do you, Leroy, take this woman to be your lawfully wedded wife? To have and to hold through sickness and health, till death do you part, so help you God?"

"I do," said Left.

The reverend then turned to Maria. "Do you take this man to be your lawfully wedded husband, to have and to hold through sickness and health, till death do you part, so help you God?"

"I do."

The reverend said, "I have been informed that you have wedding vows that you have written. Is this true?" Left and Maria nodded.

Maria's father handed her the ring. Maria put the ring on Lefts finger and said, "With this ring, I wed thee. All my life, I have been waiting for Prince Charming to come along and sweep me off my feet. I read stories about Romeo and Casanova. You may not be a Casanova or a Romeo, but you are authentic. Romeo and Casanova are only fairy tales. You are my crutch and my support. Without you, I cannot stand. From this day forward, I plan to stand with you until death do us part, so help me God." Maria's wedding vows to Left were so full of life that her mother and a few women cried. Even the good reverend had to remove his glasses and wipe his eyes with a handkerchief before anyone noticed the tears that ran down his face.

"Leroy," said the reverend.

"Yes, sir," answered Left. "Okay, Maria. Our dreams are somewhat the same. Ever since my mother passed away when I was a child, I have always felt in my heart that something was missing in my life. But now I feel complete with you, my love. I am content. It has been rough for the both of us. You put your job with the police department on the line for me, and I put my reputation and my life on the line for you. But for you, my precious queen, I will give up the breath of life."

Upon hearing this, Maria began to cry.

"Is there anyone in here who feels that these two should not be married? Speak now, or forever hold your peace," said the reverend. "Well then, with the power invested in me, I now pronounce you husband and wife. You may now kiss the bride."

Left lifted the veil on Maria's head and gave her a long, passionate kiss. Upon this, everyone clapped.

Maria's mother walked up to Maria with tears in her eyes, "My baby, my baby," she said as the two embraced. Her father and Left shook hands.

Black and the rest of Left's brothers greeted him with hugs and handshakes. "Brother, you did it," said Black as he handed Left two watch-sized boxes. "The gangsters and I bought you and Maria a little something."

Left took the two little boxes out of Black's hand. "You damn right. As little as these boxes are, it can't be anything other than 'a little something.'" Black and the crew laughed.

Black said, "Maria! Could you come over here for a minute?"

Maria walked over to where Left and the rest of the crew stood. "Yes?"

"I want you and your husband to open up the two gifts that we bought for you."

Left handed Maria one of the small boxes. Maria smiled and said, "Y'all didn't have to buy us anything. Leroy and I are grateful just to have you as friends."

"Go ahead and open them."

Left and Maria opened their gifts. "Keys?" said Left.

"I have a set of keys too," Maria said. "On the tag is an address: 2200 Brentwood Place. Hey, the chief lives over there."

"Yeah, and so do you—in your five-bedroom house," Black replied.

"I don't have a house," said Maria.

"You do now. We bought one for you two."

Maria's face lit up, and she gave Black a big hug. "Thank you all!"

"Okay, Black," said Left. "So what? My two keys go to the fence?"

Black laughed. "No, brother. Those keys go to your and Maria's new Black '79 Cadillac."

"Naw, brother," said Left as hugged all of his fellow soldiers.

"Boy, you and Maria need to come and cut this here cake," said Big Daddy. "I could use a piece right now!" Everyone laughed as they headed toward the room where the cake was.

When Left and Maria entered the room, they were greeted by Left's father. Left was not very close to him because his father hadn't been the same since Left's mother had passed away seventeen years ago. Also there was Left's oldest sister, Roxanne, who had practically raised him.

"What's up, little bro?" said Roxanne as she hugged Left and Maria.

Then Left's father embraced him. "I'm proud of you, son." Though Left and his father stood embracing each other, there was not a real bond between them, at least not the kind of bond that was supposed to be between a father and a son. Left's father hugged Maria and said, "You are so beautiful."

"Thank you, Mr. Jackson," replied Maria. "Come on, baby. Let's cut the cake."

"Okay, honey," he answered. They walked over to the cake, knife in his hand. "Here, baby." He handed Maria the knife.

The photographer stood on the opposite side of the cake from them. The tall, dark-skinned man with the camera in his hand said, "You two lovebirds let me know when you're ready."

"We are ready," said Maria.

"Okay, say cheese!"

"Cheese!" they said as the man took the picture.

With all of the dancing and toasts, time passed quickly. It was now time for Left and Maria to get started on their honeymoon. Left announced that they were leaving, and sure enough, when Left and Maria walked out of the church, there was a Cadillac parked right in front of the church with the words "Just Married" on the back window. The people threw rice at them as they walked down the steps. When Left and Maria reached the last step, Maria turned, looked at the people standing behind them, and threw the bouquet! Left opened the door for Maria to get in, and when she had pulled the tail of the dress in the car, he closed the door behind her. He then got in on the driver's side. They slowly pulled away from the church, and the crowd watched the car until it was no longer in sight.

A week later, Left and Maria returned from their honeymoon in Florida.

CHAPTER 8

As the years passed by, Truce grew, and soon it was time for her to attend preschool—but not before Left and Maria announced to all their friends that they were going to move to Florida. After hearing this, Black and the rest of the crew decided to throw them a going-away party.

"Pam, is that someone knocking on the door?" said Black in the middle of making love to Pam.

"Naw, baby," said Pam. "You know that ain't nobody coming over here on a Saturday morning."

"Maybe you are right," said Black as he and Pam started back up. Then Black heard another knock at the door. "There's that noise again, coming from the door."

"Baby, I don't hear anything."

"That's because you don't *want* to hear anything," said Black as he climbed out of bed, put his robe on, and headed for the front door.

When Black opened the door, he was met by Left. "What's up, Gangster Black?"

"What up, Left? Come on in. What made you drop by this morning?"

"Brother, you know that I couldn't leave without letting my favorite brother know."

"We were going somewhere until you knocked on the door," said Pam while standing in the doorway of the kitchen with her robe on. "As a matter of fact, I was just about to enter the land of milk and honey. I was one step away from the door. I would have been the last one of the 144,000, but someone cut out in front of me, walked through the door, and slammed it right in my face."

"I'm sorry, Pam," said Left.

"Left, don't worry about it," said Pam. "Besides, what did I lose? Nothing but streets of gold and eternal happiness." She walked back into the bedroom.

Left said, "I'm sorry, brother. I didn't mean to disrupt anything."

Black said, "Don't worry about it, Left. Pam will be all right. Hell, to be honest with you, I love it when she gets mad right before we make love. It seems like she performs better in bed when she's mad." They laughed. "So, brother, where are you two going?"

"Maria and I have decided to move to Florida, with the baby on the way. We feel that we need a fresh start, a change in location. You feel me, brother?"

"Yes, Left. You know that I feel you if nobody else does. So when do you plan on moving?"

"Monday. Maria has already gotten her job transferred to Miami."

"Damn! Bro, that's just two days away. I tell you what, Left. Tomorrow we are going to throw you a going-away party in Robert Taylor."

"Black, you don't have to throw me and Maria a party."

"Don't try to stop me, Left. Tomorrow at 10:00 a.m. Besides, it has been a long time since we've spent some time in our old hood. We have been blessed to get our own houses in good neighborhoods, but we can't act like the house negroes and forget where we came from because if we forget our past, it is more likely that we will repeat it. In order to know where we are going, we must know where we came from."

"True that, brother Black," said Left. "No one could have said it any better than that. Well, I have to go. I can't leave Maria too long by herself. She's probably finished eating those pickles and ice cream by now."

"Okay, Left. You be easy, and don't forget: tomorrow at ten o'clock."

"Okay, Black. Maria and I will be there. Just don't forget to bring my niece to the party."

"Don't worry, Left. Truce will be there."

"Peace," Left said as he walked out of the door, closing it behind him.

The next morning, Black was awakened by Pam for breakfast. "Get up, baby. It's time for breakfast." After Black washed his face, he entered the kitchen.

"Good morning, baby" Black said as he entered the kitchen. "What's for breakfast?"

"Pancakes, bacon, and oatmeal."

"Now, that's my baby. Left and Maria are moving to Florida, and I am throwing them a going-away party today at ten o'clock at Robert Taylor."

"Baby, I don't even have my hair done."

"Pam, you have almost four hours to do your hair. It's only six thirty."

"What about Truce's hair?"

"Don't even worry about that. I have already called Pimp. Shell is going to do Truce's hair. Pimp and his family will meet us at the party. Big Daddy and Big Mama are going to bring Marcus and Maurice to the party. My brothers have already bought the food, and they are going to start the grill up at eight. Big Mama stayed up all last night cooking sweet potato pies and about three or four pound cakes. Pimp also told me that Shell made a lot of banana pudding, and she also is bringing ten sweet potato pies."

"So what do you want me to cook?"

"I want you to make some potato salad."

"Well, honey, you are a little late for that," said Pam. "I made some potato salad last night, and I also baked a couple of chocolate cakes for you and the kids."

"Damn," Black said.

"What's the matter, baby?"

"I was just thinking it's a good thing that this party is for Left because if it was for anyone else, there's no way in the hell I would take those chocolate cakes over there. As a matter of a fact, we are going to leave one of those cakes here." They laughed.

After they finished eating, Black took a shower and prepared himself for the party while Pam washed the dishes. Afterward, Pam prepared herself for the event. Black and Pam wasted no time preparing themselves for the party, and they headed straight over to the Robert Taylor Housing Projects.

Upon their arrival, the sound of loud music and the smell of barbeque in the air welcomed them. One of Black's trusted soldiers, Point Blank, ran to Black's car as he spotted them pulling up. "What's up, Gangster Black?" said Point Blank.

"What's up, PB? Nothing but the struggle."

"How are you doing?" Pam asked PB.

"I'm doing just fine, ma'am," said Point Blank. "If I had a woman like you, I would give my life to the Lord."

Pam smiled upon hearing his compliment.

"Yeah? You gonna have to give your ass to me," says Black while he and Pam exited the car. The three of them burst into laughter.

"Big brother, I didn't mean any harm."

"I know, PB."

"Baby, you are still jealous after all these years?" said Pam.

"Who said I'm jealous?" responded Black as he held Pam's hand. The three of them headed toward the crowd of people beside the apartment complex.

"Look who's here!" said Point Blank.

"What's up, Gangster Black?" said Pimp as he hugged Black.

"What's up, Pimp? Did you bring some of your lord brothers with you?"

"Just a few of them, Gangster Black. Pam, how are you doing?"

"Fine, Pimp. Now, where's my daughter?"

"Truce is over there, on the sliding board."

"Truce, come here, baby," said Pam as she departed from Black and the others and headed straight to the sliding board.

"Black, you know that your right-hand man is here," said Pimp.

"Where is he? Where's Left at?"

"He's on the inside, making sure Maria doesn't need anything. You know that this is his first child, so he's kind of nervous. By now he should be tired of listening to all of that woman talk between Shell and Maria."

"Man, let me go in here and rescue my brother," Black said as he walked into the music-filled apartment. "Left, what's up, brother? Hello, Maria."

"What's up, Black? Where's Pam?" Left replied.

"She should be here in a minute. It has been about a week since Pam has had a chance to spend any time with Truce, so she's probably outside playing with her. Maria, how are you doing?"

"I'm fine. Just a few pounds heavier, but I'm fine. Baby, let's walk outside," Maria said to Left.

"Honey, you need to get some rest. I don't think that all of that moving is good for the baby."

"I know what it is. You are ashamed of me because I have lost my shape!"

"Naw, baby, I'm not ashamed of you. I love you. I'm just trying to do the right thing. But come, on, baby. Let's go outside." He helped Maria up from the couch.

Black, Pimp, Left, and Maria headed outside. Pam, Big Mama, little Truce, and all of the women were sitting at a table. Maria decided to sit with the rest of the women. The day passed by smoothly, although Left and Maria had to leave at four o'clock because they had to catch a flight to Miami, which would be leaving at five o'clock.

Black and Left said their tearful goodbyes. They had known each other for eighteen years, and this was the first time that they had ever truly been separated. Black understood that Left had a family of his own that he needed to provide for, but there was one thing for sure that Black and Left knew: no matter how far apart they were, they would always be brothers.

CHAPTER 9

"Wake up, Truce. Get up, baby," said Pam as she gently shook Truce. "It's your first day of school."

"Okay, Mama," answered Truce in a sleepy voice.

Pam then went to Marcus and Maurice. "Get up! First day of school. Breakfast is ready."

"Okay, Mama," answered Maurice.

"You too, Marcus." Pam walked back into the kitchen to see that Black had already woken up and gotten dressed.

"Good morning, baby," said Black.

"Honey, you are up early. I was going to let you sleep a little longer, at least until after I fed the kids."

"I have to go over to the barbershop and get my hair trimmed up. Big Daddy is supposed to meet me there."

"Well, baby, you know that this is Truce's first day of school. She starts preschool today."

"Pam, does she seem nervous?"

"No, honey. She seems excited. As a matter of fact, I'm the one who's nervous. Truce is handling this better than I am."

"Good morning, Daddy," said Maurice.

"Good morning, son. Good morning, Marcus."

"Morning, Dad," said Marcus.

"Morning, Daddy," Truce said as she walked into the room.

"Good morning, angel. This is your first day of school. Are you ready?"

"Yeah, Daddy, I'm ready. I can already say my ABCs."

"So what?" Maurice said.

"You're just mad because you can't say yours."

"Girl, I know my ABCs, and I can count to a hundred. I bet you can't do that, Truce."

"Leave her alone, Maurice," said Marcus.

Pam said, "Don't start that this morning, Maurice. Do you hear me?"

"Yes, ma'am."

After everyone finished eating, Pam asked Black to drop Marcus and Maurice off at school so that she could wash the dishes, put some clothes on Truce, and take her to get registered for school. "Boys, go get your book bags."

"We've already got them, Dad."

"All right, let's go. Give Mama some sugar."

Before Maurice kissed Truce, he said, "Mama, do I have to kiss Truce?"

Upon hearing this, Black and Pam burst into laughter. "That's your sister," Pam replied. "Yes, you have to kiss her."

"I don't want his ugly face kissing me. No way!" said Truce.

"I guess you heard that! Honey, quit instigating the kids."

"Daddy, do I have to kiss Truce?"

Pam said, "Boy you hear what I said?"

"Yes, ma'am." Maurice walked over and kissed Truce, who was just as unhappy as he was.

"All right, baby, we are gone," Black said as he and the boys walked out of the door.

After Pam finished cleaning the kitchen and dressing Truce for school, she and Truce headed straight over for school registration. After waiting patiently in line, they were finally called inside the school's registration office.

"May I help you?" said a rather skinny white man sitting behind a desk as they walked through the door.

"I've come to register my daughter for school."

"I'm sorry, ma'am. Would you please have a seat? Thank you. My name is Ted Black, and your name is ...?"

"Pam Williams, and this is my daughter, Truce Williams."

"May I see your ID?" Pam pulled out her driver's license and handed it to him. "You have a pretty daughter, Ms. Williams."

"Thank you."

"I see here that you are married to a Cory Williams. You have two sons, Marcus and Maurice. Is that right?"

"Yes."

"Mrs. Williams, it doesn't say here that you have a daughter."

"There must be a mistake."

"No, ma'am. This computer doesn't lie. What is your daughter's Social Security number?"

Pam gave the Social Security number.

"I'm sorry, ma'am but that is not your daughter's Social Security number. The person to whom this Social Security number belongs to is deceased. Excuse me, ma'am. Let me go out for a minute." The man walked out the door.

Pam got a bad feeling, so she walked over to the desk and picked up her driver's license. "Come on, baby. Let's go," she said as she took Truce by the hand.

Suddenly the door opened. It was the man from behind the desk along with four more people, two of them police officers. "There she is," said the man.

"Lady, please step away from the child," said the officers, who had already pulled out their guns.

"For what?" said Pam.

"Ma'am, I'm asking you to step away from the child."

"Mama, what's wrong?" said Truce, who was very confused.

Pam stepped away from Truce.

"Lady, please put your hands on the top of your head and turn around."

Pam cooperated, and one of the officers took Truce by the hand while the other one handcuffed Pam and read her her rights. The officers took them outside in front of a crowd of people. They put Pam in the back seat of one car and Truce in the front seat of another. The officer with Truce said to the other, "I'm going to take the little girl over to the children's shelter. I will meet you back at the jail."

"Ten-four."

When they arrived at the city jail, the police escorted Pam upstairs, where she was fingerprinted and given one phone call. Pam called her husband, who was shocked and upset about her being put in jail for kidnapping. Shortly after, Black and the family lawyer arrived to get her out on bond. After Pam was released on bond, the lawyer, who was the best in the state of Illinois, got the charges dropped.

For a whole year, the family went through a state of intense flux behind the removal of Truce from their family. The lawyer fought for Black to regain custody of Truce, but because of Black's reputation as a known leader of one of the most feared organizations, custody looked to be impossible.

During this tragedy, Truce was housed at the children's home. She refused to eat and was transported to a hospital, where she was fed through a tube. In the heat of all this fire, the lawyer finally broke through. There was a God! The courts allowed Big Mama visitation. Black and Pam were excited and a little upset because Big Mama was the only family member allowed to visit Truce.

Big Mama stopped by the store and bought Truce a teddy bear and some balloons.

When Big Mama arrived at the hospital, she found Truce's room vacant, but a nurse who happened to be watching her as she entered Truce's room came over to see what was going on. "Excuse me, ma'am," said the nurse to Big Mama. "May I help you?"

"Yes, I'm here to visit my granddaughter."

"Okay, you've got to be talking about little Truce. She's in the recreational room playing with the other children. I will go get her for you; wait a minute."

"Hell, I have been waiting a whole damn year just for a visit. Another minute won't kill me," Big Mama said to herself.

Sure enough, a few minutes later, Truce entered the room. When she saw Big Mama, it was as if she was running a relay race. "Big Mama, Big Mama!" Truce shouted at the top of her lungs.

"Hey, baby," Big Mama said as the two embraced each other.

"I miss you, Big Mama."

Upon hearing this, tears rushed down Big Mama's cheeks. "I miss you too, baby."

"Big Mama, are you crying?"

"Naw, baby. Big Mama's eyes are just burning. There must be dust or something floating around here. When was the last time that they cleaned your room?"

Truce laughed because she knew that Big Mama was lying.

Big Mama also laughed because she realized that Truce had seen straight through her lie. "So how's my baby been doing?"

"Fine."

"Who braided your hair for you?"

"Miss Mary."

"Who's Miss Mary?"

"She's the nurse who takes care of me. She's pretty cool. She brings me cupcakes and jelly beans."

"I brought you a little something. It's right there in that bag against the wall."

Truce ran over to the big bag. In it was a teddy bear, a robe, house shoes, and a big bag of jelly beans. "Thank you, Big Mama!"

"You are welcome."

"Big Mama?"

"Yes, baby?"

"Where's Mama and Daddy, and Marcus and Maurice? Why didn't they come with you to see me? Don't they love me anymore? Did I do something wrong?"

"Everybody still loves you. I'm just the only one they would let see you. But don't worry. Pretty soon everybody will be up here to see you."

"Where's Big Daddy at? Does he still make that ugly face when you look at him?"

"Baby, that's just the way he looks. Child, I have been looking at your grandfather's face for over forty years, and you know I still don't remember how we got married. To be honest with you, I believe that somebody hooked us up because there's no way that I would have picked him. If he was the first choice, I would have picked number two or number three."

Truce laughed until she was nearly on the floor. "Big Mama, you are so funny! Let's go to the playroom." She grabbed Big Mama by the hand and led her to the playroom. Big Mama and Truce played until they were tired.

A nurse entered the playroom. "Truce, it's time for dinner."

"Miss Mary, this is my grandma. Big Mama, this is Miss Mary." Big Mama and Miss Mary shook hands. Miss Mary was a light-skinned black woman in her midfifties with brown hair. "Miss Mary, I'm not hungry."

"Truce, you have to eat something," said Miss Mary. "Eat something for Big Mama. Will you do that for her?"

Truce nodded. After they went back into the room where Truce slept, Truce washed her hands, and Miss Mary entered the room with Truce's food in her hand. Miss Mary set the plate on a table in the corner of Truce's room. "Mrs. Williams, would you like something to eat?"

"Naw, I'd better not. I'm trying to watch my figure. I plan on going to the beach this summer." Miss Mary laughed at Big Mama.

When Truce finished eating, Miss Mary entered the room again. "Truce, it's time for you to take a bath."

"Yes, ma'am." She got herself ready to bathe. "Big Mama, I will be right back. Don't go nowhere."

"I won't." Big Mama looked at her watch: 8:30 p.m. Time had flown by—she had been at the hospital for five and a half hours. By now she was tired, but she refused to leave without telling Truce goodbye.

"Truce, it's time for you to go to bed," said Miss Mary.

"But I'm not tired."

Big Mama said, "Truce, you heard the nurse. It's time for you to go to bed. If Miss Mary doesn't mind, I will tuck you in."

"No, I don't mind."

After Big Mama put Truce to bed, Truce said to her, "Big Mama, you coming back?"

"Yeah, baby, I will be back tomorrow."

"You promise?" Big Mama leaned over and kissed Truce on the forehead. "When are they going to let me come home?"

"Soon, baby, soon. You just hang in there. We are going to get you out of this place. Okay?"

"Okay, Big Mama. I love you!"

"I love you too, baby." Big Mama walked out of the door.

Each visit, Big Mama spent hours at a time with Truce. Months passed, and the lawyer came up with a new strategy for the custody hearing. Pam was not going to be the one fighting for custody of Truce. It was going to be Big Mama. This was something that the district attorney would not be expecting.

Finally, after nearly two years, it was time for the custody hearing. The preacher and the whole congregation would be at the hearing, along with some of Big Daddy's friends from the civil rights movement. The day was here, and the courtroom was packed like a pro basketball game. The state pleaded its case, but the Williams' lawyer didn't miss a step. The lawyer acted as if he had already knew the state's strategy. The lawyer had more than twenty character witnesses.

Now it was time for the judge to make his decision, but first the judge wanted to hear what Truce had to say. The judge called Truce to the stand. One would think that a seven-year-old would crack under this kind of pressure, but Truce did the exact opposite: she stood firm and remained solid. After the judge heard all that Truce had to say concerning Big Mama and the rest of the family, he took off his glasses and laughed. "You know that it's amazing," he said. "There's no doubt in my mind that this woman is capable and qualified enough to take care of this little girl. As we all can see, this beautiful little girl loves this family. I hereby grant Glenda Williams custody of Truce Williams."

The whole courtroom cheered, and Big Mama could have sworn that she saw the DA crack a smile. This trial proved one thing for sure: the race goes neither to the swift nor the strong, but to the few who endure to the end. The Williams family had truly endured to the end.

CHAPTER 10

It was now Truce's first day of school, and she had an older sister and a cousin who would show her around: her sister and a cousin, Asia, who was Pimp's daughter, and Imani, who was Asia's cousin. Asia was about three years older than Truce, and Imani was two years older.

As young as these girls were, they were already affiliated with an organization, a black movement. Asia was following in the footsteps of her father. Therefore, she was a vice lord. Imani was a black gangster disciple, and Truce was just Truce. She had no problem with either side, and besides, it was the leaders of both organizations who had found her and taken her in.

The school bell rang, so Truce and the rest of the children headed to their classes. Immediately after Truce found the classroom she was supposed to be in, she found an empty desk in the front of the classroom and sat down. After everyone introduced themselves, the bell rang.

Soon it was lunchtime. However, Truce did not see Asia and Imani until it was time for them to go home. "Truce, girl, what's up?" said Asia. "So did you like your first day at school?"

"Well, I guess it was cool, except for one thing."

"What was that?" asked Imani.

"This boy kept smiling at me, and he acts just like my brother Maurice. I can't stand Maurice."

"Looks like you've already got a boyfriend, Truce," said Asia with a smile on her face.

A car horn blew; it was Big Daddy picking up Truce from school.

"There's my granddaddy," said Truce. "I've got to go. I will see y'all tomorrow."

"Hey, Mr. Williams," said Imani as she and Asia waved at Big Daddy.

Big Daddy smiled as he waved back at the girls. "Hello." Truce got inside the car. "Hey, baby girl. How was your first day of school?"

"It was all right, I guess, except this ugly boy kept smiling at me today. He acts just like Maurice."

"By the way, Truce, your brothers will be over for the weekend."

"Is Maurice coming, Big Daddy?"

Big Daddy laughed. "Yes, Maurice will be coming over. That's your brother. You two need to get along—you're family. Family is supposed to stick together."

When they made it to the house, Big Mama was sitting on the porch. "Hey, schoolgirl," Big Mama said. "How did your first day at school?"

"It was okay, except this ugly boy kept smiling at me."

"Well, baby, get used to it. You are going to meet a whole lot of ugly little boys. How do you think your grandfather and I first met? He was just an ugly little boy. Now he's an ugly old man, and we have two ugly sons—your dad and your uncle Frank, who's in prison."

"I heard that, Glenda," said Big Daddy.

Truce and Big Mama laughed as they walked into the house.

CHAPTER 11

The years passed, and Truce developed into a young woman. School was simple for her, and she breezed through it. The only problem that she had was trying to deal with the insufficient amount of history of black people that was being taught in her American history class. Unlike her soul sisters, Truce did not have a boyfriend to worry about. As much as Asia loved to fight, she maintained a B average in school; she could easily make straight As if she desired to do so, but Asia did only enough in school to keep her dad off her back and to keep up her weekly allowance. As for Imani, she maintained an A average along with Truce.

They were now in high school, and Asia was a senior and already drinking and smoking behind her father's back. Imani was a junior, and on rare occasions she would drink a beer or two. Imani and Truce had already set goals for their lives. Imani wanted to be a doctor, and Truce planned on becoming a lawyer. Asia was undecided.

Truce sat patiently in class, pondering over her future. She was excited because today would be the day that she would finally get a chance to meet her uncle Frank for the first time in person. He had been in prison for eighteen years. She had talked to her uncle on the phone, she had written him letters, and she had pictures of him that he had sent her from prison. But it would be nothing like meeting him face-to-face. She thought of all of the stories she had heard about her uncle and how much he loved black people.

The bell rang. "All right," said the teacher, Ms. Hambrick. "I will see you all Monday. Have a nice weekend." The students rushed out of the classroom and into the hallway—everyone except Truce and one young man, who appeared to be waiting at the door for her.

"Hello, Truce. How are you doing?"

"Fine. I'm just trying to get settled in."

"Truce, you have a very beautiful name."

"Thank you. My dad gave it to me."

"I'm sorry," said the young man as he followed Truce to her locker. "I forgot to tell you my name. My name is Eric."

"Brother," said Truce while placing her hands on her hips, "that was a poor pickup line, especially if you are trying to score. Personally, I'm not interested, but you are going to have to do better than that if you plan on scoring."

Eric, who was a sophomore, had never heard any of the other girls talk as boldly as Truce. "I wasn't trying to score with you."

"Good, because you didn't," Truce said with a smile on her face.

Just as Eric began to comment, Asia and Imani walked up. "Damn, li'l' sis," said Asia. "This is your first year of high school, and you're already marking your territory."

Truce said, "Eric, these are my two sisters, Imani and Asia."

"What's up, Eric?" said Asia. "How would you like to take my little sister to the party?"

"Girl," Truce warned.

"I'm game," said Eric. "Would you like to go out with me, Truce?"

"Yes, brother, she would love to go out with you," said Asia.

"I can speak for myself, girl." Upon hearing Truce's remarks, Asia and Imani burst into laughter. Even Truce and Eric began to laugh. "Eric, let me think about it for a couple of days. I will let you know Monday, okay?"

"Nice meeting you two," Eric said to Imani and Asia as he disappeared into the crowded hallway.

"Damn," said Asia. "Girl, you've got the best-looking man in the school sweating, and you are playing hard to get! You'd better let that kitty cat out of the cage."

"Asia, I'm waiting on the right man."

"How do you know if he's the right man if you don't give him a chance?"

Imani said, "Asia, lay off her. Truce has her whole life ahead of her. When the time is right, she will choose a man."

"Yeah, big sister. I have my whole life ahead of me."

"Okay, little sister," Asia said. "Girls, let's get the hell out of here."

As the three exited the school, Asia bumped into one of her rival enemies, Carla, who was talking to a small crowd of girls standing next to her car. As Asia passed by Carla, Carla looked Asia up and down and said, "I hate it."

"That's all right. Your ex-nigger likes it—all of it."

"Bitch, you ain't shit," said Carla.

Imani pulled a switchblade out of her purse and said to Truce, "Get in the car."

"No," answered Truce. "If it's going down, I'm riding with y'all."

"Girl, I don't have time to be arguing with your little ass. There's a bat under the seat."

"Who you calling a bitch?" Asia said to Carla.

"You, bitch."

Upon that remark, Asia slapped Carla, and the two tied up. Imani ran around the car and warned the rest of Carla's clique to not get in it. Truce stood at four feet eleven, and she watched from the other side of the car with a baseball bat in her hand.

"Girl, kick her ass!" said Imani. "Whip that bitch's ass."

Asia and Carla wrestled all over the cars of the parking lot. The two fell on the ground and punched each other in the face. All the rest of Carla's girls finally jumped in. Truce ran from behind the car with the bat in her hand and went straight to work without hesitation. The other females began to disappear, and finally Imani got back up on her feet and went toe-to-toe with this other sister. She seemed to be the most loyal to Carla. Asia continued to pound on Carla, whose face was bloody.

Imani had her hands full with the girl she was fighting. Somehow, Imani grabbed a handful of her hair, flipped the girl on her back, and stomped her. The girl let Imani know that she had had enough by balling up on the ground. Truce tried to pull Asia off Carla, who was no longer putting up a fight. "Asia, let her go. Imani, help me!"

Imani rushed over to help Truce. "Girl, let her go," said Imani while she and Truce pulled Asia off Carla. Finally, Asia gave in and let go of Carla.

By that time, someone told Maurice that his little sister was fighting in the parking lot. Maurice and ten of his brothers made an entrance by firing a shot in the air. That made the crowd of people hit the ground. "What's up, baby sister?" said Maurice with a small pistol in his hand.

"Boy, put that gun up before someone gets hurt."

"Damn that—point their asses out!"

Sirens went off. The police were entering the school parking lot.

"Let's go!" said Asia. She and the rest of the crew got inside of the car and pulled away. Maurice and his clique faded into the crowd of other students.

Asia dropped Truce off at home. Truce said, "Girl, y'all call me when you get home, okay?"

As Truce entered the house, she was greeted by her uncle Frank and the rest of her family—everyone except Maurice. "Is that my niece?" said a tall dark-skinned man standing next to Big Mama. "Uncle Frank in the flesh," he said, coming to meet Truce.

Truce hugged and kissed Frank on the cheek. "Girl, you gonna be a real heartbreaker."

"Hold it right there," said Big Mama. "Let me grab the camera." She exited the living room while Truce hugged Black.

"What's up, Daddy?"

"You're precious," Black replied.

"I'm back," said Big Mama cheerfully with a camera in her hand. "Okay, Frank. You and Truce are going to take the first picture." Truce and Frank posed for a picture. "The next picture will be Big Daddy, Frank, Black, and Marcus. After that will be me and the rest of the family."

Sherryl was Big Mama's Wednesday-night bingo partner and also her best friend.

"Where's li'l' Maurice at?" asked Frank.

"That boy will be late for his own funeral," said Pam. Everyone laughed.

"Mama, that's Maurice pulling up outside," said Truce.

"Boy, come on before you miss taking the picture," hollered Big Mama at Maurice.

"Glenda," said Big Daddy, "the boy's just outside, not down the street."

"Okay, honey," said Big Mama while putting a little smile on her face. It was the kind of smile that a little girl had when she had a crush.

"What's up in here?" said Maurice as he walked through the door.

Big Mama looked at Big Daddy with a smile on her face. "Those are your grandchildren, and all of them are crazy."

"Y'all ain't gonna rest until you run Truce crazy." Upon hearing Big Daddy's remarks, everyone laughed!

"What's up, nephew?"

"You must be Uncle Frank," said Maurice as they embraced each other.

"Come on," said Big Mama. "Let's take a picture of the whole family. Sherryl, you ready?"

"Yes, Glenda. Come on, y'all."

Big Daddy said, "Let's take this picture before your grandmother's blood pressure goes up."

After Sherryl took the picture, everyone headed to the kitchen to eat dinner. When they sat at the table, Big Mama said, "Who's going to bless the food?"

"How about Uncle Frank?" said Truce.

"Okay, son," said Big Daddy. "Come on with it."

"Let us bow our heads," said Frank. Everyone bowed their heads except for Frank. Frank didn't believe in slipping. He also believed he could get caught slipping while he was praying. "We thank you, God, for making our family complete again. Without you, none of this would be possible because you are the creator of the heavens and the earth and the provider for the world. Amen."

CHAPTER 12

On Sunday morning, the whole family was going to church together for the first time in eighteen years. Big Mama was up cooking breakfast, humming gospel songs. Today was going to be a big day. Truce was going to be leading the choir.

"Breakfast! Everybody, get up for breakfast," said Big Mama as she walked from door to door, waking everybody up. After everyone woke and took care of their personal hygiene, they ate breakfast. After that, they all got dressed for church and loaded up in the family car, which was a 1985 Cadillac Seville.

Upon the Williams family entering the church, all the elders of the church were happy to see Frank. Truce was happy to see her two sisters, Asia and Imani. "Girl," said Asia as she and Imani walked over and hugged Truce, "who is that fine brother who walked in with y'all?"

"That's my uncle Frank."

"I would love to be your aunt," said Asia.

"True that," said Imani.

"Y'all want to meet him?" Truce said. "Uncle Frank, come over here for a minute."

"Girl, don't call him over here!" said Asia.

"What up, baby girl?"

"Uncle Frank, these are my two sisters, Asia and Imani."

"Pleased to meet you, Asia. Imani, pleased to meet you."

"Truce has told us all about you," said Imani. "Truce told us that you were part of the movement when you were thirteen years old."

Frank laughed. "What else did my niece tell you, Imani?"

"Truce said that you were a revolutionary and also a black nationalist."

"I'm a black realist," Frank replied with a smile on his face as he walked away. "Oh, girls," said Frank as he turned around. "I almost forgot something."

"What is it, Uncle Frank?"

"I'm still a part of the movement—and don't you forget that, baby girl."

"Truce," said Big Mama.

"Yes?"

"Mr. Parks is looking for you. The choir is ready to begin."

"Y'all, I've got to sing."

"Go ahead, girl, with your bad self."

Truce joined the rest of the choir behind the pulpit. "Waiting on you, Truce," said Mr. Parks.

"Sorry, Mr. Parks."

"That's okay. One, two, three," Mr. Parks said as he gave the choir the cue. The choir began to sing, following Truce's lead.

"If anyone should ask you where I'm going soon, if anyone should ask you where I'm going soon, I beg you tell them to be with my Lord! I'm going up yonder, going up yonder, going up yonder to be with my Lord!" Truce sang with style.

Asia listened to Truce sing her favorite song, as wild as Asia seemed, there were tears in her eyes, clearly proving that there was a soft spot in her heart.

After the choir finished the song, Truce joined her two sisters in the second row as the Reverend Ben Woods took his place behind the podium to give the sermon. Over the twenty-five years that Reverend Woods had been preaching, it had been said that he had never preached a boring sermon.

After church was over, the Williams family paid their respects to everyone, and when everyone had eaten, the Williams family returned to their home.

CHAPTER 13

Truce finished her breakfast as someone honked a horn outside. Big Mama looked through the curtains. "Truce, the girls are here to pick you up for school."

"Okay," Truce said as she kissed Big Mama on the cheek. "I will see you when I get back from school."

"Okay, baby girl."

Truce closed the door behind her. As she approached the car, Asia and Imani greeted her with a warm welcome. "What's up, girl? So are you going to give that fine-ass nigga some play?" Asia said.

"What the hell. I might as well give Eric a chance."

"That's my girl," said Asia as Truce got in the car. "Girl, you sang your ass off yesterday at church."

"You think so?"

"Imani, did the girl blow up yesterday at church, or what?"

"Hell yeah. Girl, you sounded like Mahalia Jackson." As they pulled into the school parking lot, Eric was standing on the curb and talking to some students.

"Eric! Hey, Eric!" Asia screamed through the car window while she was parking.

Eric approached the car with a smile on his face. "Where's Truce?"

"She's in the back," said Asia. "Eric, my little sister likes you, but she's too shy tell you."

"Asia, I can speak for myself."

"Excuse me, baby girl. Imani, you hear that? Baby girl says that she can speak for herself. Imani, open the door and let Ms. Thang's hot ass out."

As Truce stepped out of the car, she said, "Don't pay them fools no attention."

"I'm not. Can I carry your books for you?"

"Naw, brother. If Marcus saw you carrying my books, he would probably want to kick your ass."

"I'm not worried about anyone doing that. By the way, Truce, who's Marcus?"

"My brother—Marcus O. Williams."

"Crazy Marcus Williams, disciple?"

"Yes, that's him."

"Girl, your brother and I are tight."

"Trust me, Eric. Y'all are not that tight. As a matter of fact, there's that fool now, standing by the door."

Marcus and three more students came out to meet them. "What's up, baby girl?"

"Nothing, bro."

"What's up, my man, Marcus?" Eric said.

"It depends, nigger. If you are trying to talk to my sister, your ass may be on the back of one of those milk cartons."

"Marcus, I talk to who I want to. You are not my dad, and you can't run my life. Come on, Eric. Let's go," said Truce as she grabbed Eric by the arm. Class was about to begin. Truce and Eric walked to Truce's locker.

"Truce, you know that I like you."

"Please don't go there. We can be friends."

"Something wrong with me?"

"I didn't say that. Brother, I'm not interested in a relationship."

"Cool, I respect that. But if you change your mind ..."

"Don't worry—I won't."

The bell rang, and students came in from outside. "Eric, I have to go to class."

"Truce, I would like to have lunch with you."

"That's cool."

While Truce was in English class, it was very hard for her to stay focused on class. Her mind was on Eric. She had to admit that Eric was attractive. After pondering over how far she was going to let her friendship go with Eric, Truce finally convinced herself that there was nothing wrong with having a boyfriend.

The bell rang, and it was time for lunch. After the teacher reminded the students that there would be a test tomorrow, she dismissed them from class. When Truce entered the hallway, Eric was standing by her locker, waiting.

"Hey, precious," said Eric. "Are you ready?"

"Yeah. Let me put my books in my locker."

Truce and Eric walked into the crowed lunchroom, which sounded like a high school pep rally. They walked through the line, got their trays, and went to a table. Truce set her lunch tray on the table.

"Hold it, Truce," said Eric as he pulled out her chair for her.

"Thank you, Eric."

"You are welcome, precious. So how was your weekend?"

"It was fine. I went to church with my girls. I was the lead singer in the choir."

"Oh, yeah? What did you sing?"

"'Going Up Yonder.'"

"That's one of my favorite gospel songs."

"Brother, you don't have to lie to kick it."

"Precious, I'm not lying."

"Come on, Eric. Let's go. I have to go to social studies class."

Truce and Eric were spotted by Asia and Imani. "Baby girl!" screamed Asia across the lunchroom as she and Imani quickly moved to meet them. "Now, that's what I'm talking about! My little sister is making a claim."

"Asia, you need to quit," Truce warned. "Eric and I are just friends."

"So what you are telling us," said Imani, "is that there's nothing going on between you and Eric."

"What I'm telling you is that it's none of your business."

"Okay, Miss Thang," said Asia. "Excuse me for getting in your business."

Truce and Eric left Asia and Imani in the lunchroom.

CHAPTER 14

As the months passed by, Truce and Eric went out on date after date, and they grew closer. What used to be a kiss in the morning and after school became a kiss every time they saw each other. Even Marcus began to lighten up on Eric, but Marcus always reminded Eric that if he ever hurt his little sister, Marcus would kill him. As for Maurice, he didn't know about Eric. Maurice had joined the navy and had been sent to Germany. No one told him that Truce had a boyfriend because they knew it would upset him.

Minute by minute, the relationship grew stronger. Eric began to ask Truce when she was going to have sex with him. Truce was a virgin and didn't know what to expect. Big Mama had told Truce that she only should have sex after she got married, but she received advice from her sisters—especially Asia, who had been having sex since the eighth grade. After wrestling with herself, Truce finally decided to have sex with Eric.

It was Thursday night, and Truce was in bed thinking about tomorrow night. Only God knew how nervous she was. Truce fell asleep with thoughts of Eric on her mind. The night passed quickly.

Big Mama got up before the rest of the family and cooked breakfast as always, but she no longer prepared a big breakfast because Frank had moved into his own place. After Big Mama finished cooking breakfast, she woke up Big Daddy and Truce.

Everyone finished eating, and Big Mama washed the dishes and cleaned up the kitchen.

"Truce," said Big Mama, "when are you going to let me meet Eric?"

"Tonight. He will be over here to pick me up. We're going to the movies, if that's all right with you."

"Yeah, baby. You can go to the movies—just as long as you're back home by eleven thirty."

Big Daddy said, "Well, Truce, can I go to the movies with you? The last time that I went to the movies, it was only a nickel."

"Honey, the last time we went to the movies, it wasn't called a movie; it was called a picture show." Upon hearing this, Truce laughed.

"So, Truce, can I tag along with you?"

"No, Big Daddy. Eric and I are going by ourselves."

"You ashamed of your granddaddy? I won't cramp your style."

Truce hugged Big Daddy and gave him a big kiss.

"Girl, I used to change you diapers. I used to push you in the swing. I bought you your first bicycle. And this is the thanks that I get?"

"Truce, don't pay your granddaddy any attention."

A car horn honked outside, and Truce looked out of the door. "It's Asia. I will see you when I get back." She closed the door behind her, then she walked outside and got into the car with her sister.

"What's up, baby girl?" said Asia.

"The struggle," answered Truce.

"True that," responded Imani. "So what are you doing tonight?"

"Eric and I are getting together tonight."

"Are you going to give it to Eric tonight?"

"That's none of your business."

Asia and Imani burst into laughter; even Truce laughed.

As they entered the school parking lot, the girls spotted Eric sitting on the hood of his car.

Asia parked beside Eric's car. "Your baby's in the back seat. Open the door, Imani. Baby girl, Eric isn't going anywhere."

"What's up, baby?" said Eric as Truce got out of the car.

"Nothing," responded Truce. The two embraced each other and shared a warm, intimate kiss.

"Damn, baby girl, you are going to eat the brother up," said Imani as she and Asia walked away laughing.

"Don't pay them any attention," said Eric.

"I'm not."

"So, are we on for tonight?"

"Yes, Eric. My grandmother wants to meet you, and I'm telling you now: don't pay my grandfather any attention. He's going to be teasing you."

"Don't worry about it, baby. I can handle it." The school bell rang. "Come on, baby. Let's get to our classes before we are late."

They walked into the school. The hallways were filled with students rushing to their classes. Truce and Eric kissed before departing for their separate classes. Truce made it to class just in time for the English test.

"Everyone, please put up everything except for your pencil. I hope that you studied for the test." Ms. Simpson was a very dedicated teacher who took pride in teaching. She had been born in the fifties. She also remembered how hard it was for blacks to get a good education in the sixties and seventies.

Truce finished taking the test, although it was very difficult because Eric was on her mind. After tonight, she would no longer be the same. If her brother Maurice found out about her and Eric's plans, Eric's life would never be the same either because Marcus probably would kill Eric.

The bell rang; it was time for lunch. Truce followed her regular routine and met Eric in the hallway. They shared an intimate kiss before going to the lunchroom. After they finished eating, the two departed, but not before Eric got reassurance from her that their date was still on for tonight.

The day passed very quickly. After Asia took Truce home from school, Truce spent the rest of the day watching the clock. It was six thirty; in an hour and a half, Eric would be knocking on the door. Truce decided to take a shower and get prepared for the big night—a night that she would forever remember. After Truce had taken a bath, she got dressed, turned on a little jazz, and sat anxiously on the side of her bed waiting for Eric. Time passed as Truce sat and listened to the music flow though the speakers.

Big Mama opened the door and said, "Baby girl?"

"Yes, ma'am," answered Truce.

"There is a fine young man in the living room looking for you."

"That's Eric. How does my hair look?"

"Baby girl, you look fine. You'd better go out there before your grandfather asks Eric a thousand questions."

Truce hurried into the living room, but it was too late—Big Daddy had already moved in on Eric. When Big Daddy noticed that Truce and Big Mama were staring at him, he included them in the conversation. "Hey, baby girl. Eric and I were just getting to know each other. Honey, have you met Eric? Come on in here and meet him."

Big Mama and Truce walked into the living room. Big Mama said, "You kids have a good time."

Upon hearing this, Truce kissed Big Daddy on the cheek, grabbed Eric by the hand, and exited. "I will be back at eleven thirty. Don't wait up for me!" She closed the door behind her.

Big Daddy turned and looked at Big Mama. "Glenda, why did you do that?"

"Honey, Truce is growing up. You can't be overprotective."

"That's my granddaughter, and I will be overprotective of her as long as I'm living. Now, Glenda, do we have some ice cream in the refrigerator?"

"Yes, we have some chocolate and vanilla ice cream."

"Do we have some black walnut?"

"No, honey," said Big Mama. "I didn't know that you liked black walnut."

"Well, I do," said Big Daddy as he removed his coat from the coat hanger.

"Where are you going?"

"I'm going to the store to get some black walnut ice cream."

"No, you're not! You are going to try to follow Truce and Eric!"

"No, I'm not, honey."

"If Truce finds out that you are following her and Eric, she will be very upset."

"Okay, Glenda, I guess you are right." Big Daddy put his coat back on the hanger. Big Mama kissed Big Daddy.

Meanwhile, Truce and Eric bypassed the movie theater. Truce looked at the movie theater. Eric approached the parking lot of a park that appeared to be closed, and Truce took another deep breath.

Eric parked beside a bicycle rack. "We are here," he said.

"Eric, what if the police come?"

"That's all right. The park stays open all night. Finally, baby, we are alone." Eric leaned over and kissed Truce.

The butterflies in Truce's stomach stirred. Next, Eric blew in Truce's ear. The butterflies that were in Truce's stomach left. Truce's heart now burned with passion as Eric opened her top. Truce took off Eric's shirt. Then Eric gently laid Truce down on the seat as he kissed her breast. Eric pulled off his pants, and Truce pulled off hers. Truce began to squirm as Eric penetrated her.

"Hold up, Eric!" said Truce.

"I will be gentle."

Truce shivered as she reached ecstasy. Thoughts went through her head as she lay her head on Eric's chest. Her life would never be the same again.

CHAPTER 15

On Sunday morning, Big Mama sang as she prepared breakfast for the family. Truce would be leading the choir at church again. As Big Mama pulled the biscuits out of the oven, she announced to her family that it was breakfast time. Big Mama knew that the other two were hard sleepers, so she walked to each door and hollered for them to get up for breakfast. Shortly after, Big Daddy and Truce entered the kitchen.

"Good morning," said Big Mama. Both replied in low, sleepy voices. "Who's going to bless the food?"

"You," answered Truce and Big Daddy.

"Well, okay, I will bless the food."

After breakfast was over, Big Mama reminded Truce that she had to sing in church today. "Truce, I hope that you are ready to sing."

"Yes, ma'am."

Everybody prepared for church. Big Daddy was the first one dressed, so he went outside to listen to some blues before the girls got in the car. After Big Daddy listened to a song or two, the others arrived. Big Daddy turned off the music, got out of the car, and opened the car door for them like a real gentlemen. "So how are my favorite two women doing this morning?"

"Ask her!" snapped Big Mama.

"Truce, what's going on between you and your grandma?"

"I don't want to talk about it," Truce said as she rolled her eyes.

"Girl, I know you didn't just roll your eyes at me."

"Ladies, ladies, hold it. Truce, what have you done, young lady? I haven't seen your grandmother this mad in a long time. She hasn't been this upset in about thirty years. Well, we are here now at the Lord's house, so you ladies put this on hold until after church is over."

"How could you be so stupid? What I tell you goes in one ear and out the other."

"Glenda, knock it off, honey." Big Daddy opened the door for Big Mama. "Glenda, I want to talk to you. Truce, go on in the church; we'll be there in a little while."

Truce walked into the church and was welcomed by everyone in the church, especially her father Black, who had a smile on his face like a child who had just received an ice-cream cone.

"Hey, baby. How are you doing?" Black said as he hugged Truce and kissed her forehead. "Your mother and I were wondering when you were going to come over and spend some time with us. Maurice is gone to the army. We miss hearing you and Marcus arguing."

"Well, Dad, I'm sorry that I haven't been over to see you and Mama. With school and a few more things in my life, I have been kind of busy."

"A few more things? Like what? Don't tell me that you have a boyfriend or something."

Upon hearing this, Truce laughed. "Well, Daddy, I know what you told me about having a boyfriend, but I met this brother named Eric, and I really like him."

"Pam, Pam!" Black said. "Come over here and listen to what your daughter has to say."

"Hey, baby," said Pam as she greeted Truce with a kiss. "We are waiting to hear you sing."

"Mom, Dad called you over here for me to tell you about my boyfriend."

"When am I going to get the chance to meet him?"

"Meet him?" Black repeated. "I wish that he would come over here."

"Truce, don't pay your dad any attention. Now go on and get ready to sing."

"Okay, Mama. I hope you like my singing," said Truce as she walked over to join the rest of the choir.

"Girl, don't play with me," Black responded to Truce's sarcastic statement.

"Honey, leave her alone," Pam said. "We met in the eighth grade, and we have been together for twenty years."

"Pam, let's grab a seat, because you are going to take sides with her."

Black and Pam sat down in the third row of seats. Asia and Imani sat in the front row, patiently waiting to hear their sister lead the choir. They also wanted an opportunity to tease her about her sinful acts of fornication that she had committed Friday night with Eric.

Truce grabbed the microphone and prepared to lead the choir in a very old and popular Negro spiritual, "Soon and Very Soon." As Truce started the song, Big Daddy and Big Mama walked through the door. Big Mama's mouth was poked out like a teenage girl who was mad at her teenage boyfriend. But Big Mama wasn't a teenage girl—she was Truce's grandmother.

As the choir instructor gave the cue, Truce led the song. "Soon and very soon, we are going to see the King. Hallelujah, hallelujah, we are going to see the King."

While Truce sang, Asia and Imani began to tease her. "It's not the king that everybody else is talking about, but King Eric," said Imani.

"Little heifer has got some nerve," said Asia. "Heifer's going to bust hell wide open."

Truce tried to hold her laugh while singing. After the choir finished the song, everybody in the church stood up and applauded. Truce walked over to greet her two sisters, and the three of them laughed. Truce chanced a look at Big Mama, who had a small smirk on her face, but when Big Mama noticed that Truce was looking at her, she wiped the smirk off her face and began to poke her mouth back out. No matter how mad Big Mama got, she could not hide how much she loved to hear her granddaughter sing.

After Reverend Ben Woods preached his fiery sermon and everyone ate, the Williams family loaded up in the car and went home. It was a long, quiet ride home; no one said a word.

Big Daddy decided to initiate a conversation. "Baby girl, that was some mighty fine singing."

"Thank you, Big Daddy," Truce said as she kissed him on the cheek.

"What you think about your granddaughter's singing, Glenda?" said Big Daddy.

"Don't ask me anything about that hardheaded girl," said Big Mama.

Poor Truce felt lower than an ant crawling on the ground.

Finally, they made it home. Big Daddy opened the door for Big Mama and Truce. When they walked inside the house, he said, "Well, I'm going to bed."

After he went into his room and closed the door behind him, Big Mama spoke to Truce. "Come on. Let's go sit on the porch. I want to talk to you." She led the way to the porch swing and sat down. "Sit down, baby. Honey, I didn't mean to come down on you so hard, but what you did is more serious than you think. Sex can be beautiful when performed under the right condition. When two people love each other and have made vows and a commitment under God and the laws that he established for the unification and marriage for a man and woman, then sex is beautiful. But when you do it because some of the other girls in high school are doing it, that's plain stupid and dangerous. It's not like you don't know any better. I've had talks with you about sex a lot of times. Did he ejaculate in you?"

"No, ma'am."

"When you have unprotected sex, you are taking a chance at catching all types of sexually transmitted diseases. You can even get pregnant. If you get pregnant, I'm going to kill you, because I'm not ready to be a great-grandmother. I'm not old enough to be a great-grandmother." Big Mama and Truce laughed while they embraced each other on the swing.

CHAPTER 16

As the years passed by, Truce and Eric grew even closer. A lot of things were happening. Asia and Imani had graduated. Imani had gone off to medical school in Virginia, and Asia became a mother. The beautiful thing about it was that Asia named her daughter after Truce. Truce's mother and father had moved to Alabama.

Truce was now a senior. She had made up her mind that she was going to law school to be a district attorney. A few colleges had already offered her full scholarships. There was only one thing in her life that troubled her, and she would give anything to change the situation: Big Daddy's health. He had already had two slight heart attacks.

"Truce," said Big Mama as she knocked on the door of her room. "Get up. It's time for breakfast."

After Truce washed her face and brushed her teeth, she entered the kitchen. "Good morning," she said as she kissed Big Daddy on the cheek.

"This is your last year of school. Have you decided where you are going to go to college and what you are going to major in?"

"Now, Big Daddy, I haven't decided where I want to go to college, but I want to be a district attorney."

"Baby, that's going to cost me a lot of money. What are you trying to do, make me have another heart attack?"

Upon hearing Big Daddy's humorous statement, Big Mama and Truce burst into laughter.

"No, Gramps. I have been offered a few full scholarships."

"They are not going to pay for you to go to law school."

"Well, let me get ready for school," Truce said as she left the table with a smile on her face.

"We need to sell your car so that we will have a little money to help with your college."

"Honey, stop teasing her."

"Glenda, do you know how much money that I paid for that car?" Big Mama simply smiled without saying a word. "That's what I thought. Glenda, you are always saying yes to whatever she asks for, but I always end up paying for it."

"Well, that's your granddaughter."

"I know what I am going to do, baby girl. Come out here for a minute."

"Yes?" Truce said as she entered the kitchen with an arm full of books.

"You are grounded!"

"For what?"

"I don't know, but I will think of something. Now, give me the keys to your car."

"Baby girl, go ahead and leave," said Big Mama.

Truce walked over and kissed Big Mama on the cheek and Big Daddy on the forehead. Then she exited the door. She went to Eric's house to pick him up so that she could drop him off at work on her way to school. Eric worked down the street from Truce's school at a department store.

Finally, Truce arrived at Eric's house. Eric lived in a middle-class neighborhood, just as she did. Truce honked the horn as she pulled in the driveway of Eric's house. Eric exited the door with a smile on his face. "What's up, baby?" he said as he got in. Next, he gave Truce a warm, passionate kiss.

"Hold up, brother. I've got to get to school."

"If we start up this mess, you are going to be late for school, and I am going to be late for work."

"My gramps already wants to repossess my car."

"Hold up, baby. You are going to pass my job."

"Believe me, brother, I'm not going to pass your job," said Truce as she stopped in front of the department store. "Uncle Frank's girlfriend is a teacher at my school. If she sees you in this car with me this early in the morning, she is going to tell my uncle, and he is going to blow things out of proportion. Give me a kiss."

Eric kissed Truce and said, "Baby, you are so cold," as he closed the car door.

Truce pulled into the school parking lot. She received dirty looks from Rholanda, a girl who was rumored to be sleeping with Eric. Truce did not pay those rumors any attention. Eric was one of the sexiest brothers in the whole Windy City, and there were a lot of girls who would love to get their hands on him. Truce politely got out of her car, closed the door behind her, and smiled at Rholanda. "What's up?"

Rholanda put on a fake smile and then she responded. "Nothing, girl. Just waiting to go to college next year."

"What about marrying Eric?" said Truce as she headed toward the school's front door. She entered the school walking like an Egyptian queen. A lot of the boys were watching Truce with sparkles in their eyes. She had put on about ten pounds in all the right places, although she was still small in size compared to the other girls at school. Truce also received some dirty looks from some girls whose boyfriends were sweating her.

Truce read the schedule on the wall to see where her classes were. Truce had Ms. Johnson for history this year, and she was looking forward to it. Ms. Johnson had a reputation for being the best black history teacher in the state. She dealt with the most controversial subjects—subjects that other history teachers stayed away from. It was also a great possibility that Ms. Johnson was

Truce's future aunt. Truce's Uncle Frank and Miss Johnson had been living together almost since Frank had gotten out of prison.

After Truce went to her first class, which was English, everything else seemed to pass by smoothly. Finally, it was time for her to meet Ms. Johnson. Truce entered the classroom with a smile on her face. When Ms. Johnson saw Truce, she seemed to have a smile on her face. "Everyone, please be seated," said Ms. Johnson. The whole classroom became quiet. "My name is Ms. Johnson. I will be your history teacher this semester. I don't know about history, but I do know that if you have an open mind and if you participate, you will learn something. I don't know what you are going to do in your other classes, but in my class, we are going to be one big family, a close family—very close. In order for us to be a close family, we have to get to know each other. Therefore we are going to stand up and tell the class our names, starting with me. My name is Evet Johnson, but if anyone calls me by my first name, I will give you enough homework to last you until you are my age."

"How old are you, Ms. Johnson?" asked a boy who was sitting beside Truce.

"None of your business," answered Ms. Johnson. "Since you have all of the questions, we are going to let you be the first one to introduce yourself to the class."

"My name is Fred Kent."

"Next," said Ms. Johnson.

"My name is Rholanda Huges."

After the rest of the class introduced themselves, Ms. Johnson called Truce to stand up and introduce herself.

Truce stood up and said, "Hello, my name is Truce Williams."

After that, it was time for lunch. "Everybody, go to lunch," said Ms. Johnson. The students quickly exited the classroom.

"Excuse me, Ms. Williams," Ms. Johnson said to Truce before she exited.

"Yes, ma'am."

"Are you related to Frank Williams?"

"He's my uncle."

"I thought that Frank had shown me some pictures of you. Anyway, Truce, Frank has told me a lot about you. He said that you love black history."

"Yes, ma'am, I do. Uncle Frank told you that?"

"Yes. How else would I know this? I'm not a part of the CIA." Truce laughed. "Frank also told me that you want to be a district attorney."

"Yes, ma'am. I am going to get all of the drugs out of the black communities. I am going to bring down all of this organized crime bosses. Ms. Johnson, Uncle Frank also told me a lot about you."

"What did he tell you about me?"

"He said that besides my grandmother and me, he has never loved a woman the way that he loves you."

"Frank said that about me?"

"Yes, ma'am."

"Well, when are you going to come over and spend a weekend with us?"

"Ms. Johnson, you know I am very busy, but I am going to come over and spend the week with you just as soon as I get some free time."

"All right. I am going to tell Frank that I saw you."

"Okay, Ms. Johnson. You do that," Truce said as she walked through the door.

The rest of the day breezed by, and it was time for Truce to go home. She headed toward the door that led to the student parking lot. There were a lot of guys gazing at her as she quickly moved through the hallway.

When Truce made it to the parking lot, Rholanda and a group of girls were standing beside her car. "Girl, we were just standing here checking out your car," said Rholanda. "Truce, that's a sharp-ass Cadillac, and it's my favorite color, black."

"Thank you, Rholanda," Truce said as she opened the door, rolled down the window, and closed the door behind her.

"You know what they say about black? Black is beautiful. Truce, go on with your bad self," replied Rholanda.

"Excuse me, Truce," said another girl standing with Rholanda.

"Yeah, what's up?"

"Are you and Eric still kickin' it?"

"Every time we get the chance," Truce replied while turning the ignition. "Hey, girls, I hate to be a party pooper, but I have to go—Eric is waiting on me to pick him up."

"Well, Truce, I will see you tomorrow."

"Okay, Rholanda." Truce turned up the volume on her radio before pulling away.

Rholanda and her clique watched Truce as her car exited the school parking lot. "I can't stand that little bitch," Rholanda said. "Eric said that he was going to dump her ass for me. I don't know how much longer I can wait. I am tired of having to sneak around with Eric. The more that we have sex, the more that I become attached to him. I might have to run her ass away myself."

CHAPTER 17

It was Friday evening, and Truce was on her way home from school. She had just dropped off Eric at his house, and her day seemed to be going fine. But as she pulled up at the house, all that changed. Curiosity immediately began to take over. There was an ambulance parked in the driveway, and the paramedics were bringing someone out. *Who is it?* she thought. Truce parked by the curb, jumped out of the car, and headed over to see who was being loaded into the ambulance. By that time, Big Mama had come out of the door with her purse in her hand.

"Grandma!" Truce yelled. "Is it Granddaddy?"

"Yes, baby. He had a heart attack."

"Granddaddy!" screamed Truce as she grabbed the side of the stretcher.

"Excuse me, young woman. Please step back," said one of the paramedics.

"Baby, call Frank and tell him to meet us at the hospital."

"Yes, ma'am." Truce watched as the ambulance pulled away with the two most important people in her life in the back of it. Would Big Daddy make it through the heart attack? She hurried into the house to call Frank.

After Truce informed Frank of Big Daddy's heart attack, she got into her car. She had never even tried to drive fast. If Big Daddy knew that Truce was speeding in her car, he would make them stop the ambulance just so he could ground her. Thoughts raced through her head while she drove to the hospital—thoughts that she did not want to think.

Upon entering the hospital's parking lot, she saw Uncle Frank and Ms. Johnson walking toward the hospital entrance. Truce honked her horn to get their attention, but Frank did not even look back to see who was blowing the horn. His main focus was on his father, who was fighting for his life. After Truce parked her car, she entered the hospital and headed straight to the emergency room. The closer she got to the emergency room, the more she heard crying. When Truce made it to the waiting room, she saw Big Mama crying in Frank's arms.

"Big Mama, is Big Daddy all right?"

"No," answered Marcus, who was standing beside Ms. Johnson. "He didn't make it."

"No! No!" screamed Truce as she burst into tears. "Why? Why?"

Marcus walked over and put his arms around Truce—something that he hadn't done since she was a little girl. This proved that he loved his little sister regardless of their differences. While Truce and Big Mama cried, Black and Pam walked in and received the bad news. The whole family, except Maurice, stood in the waiting room mourning the loss of their loved one.

CHAPTER 18

It seemed that the deaths of well-respected and loved individuals caused people to come together. The death of Big Daddy brought people from far and near. Maurice came home from the military to attend his grandfather's funeral. Left and Maria came from Florida; it had been nearly seven years since Left and Maria had last visited Chicago. There were a lot of members of the civil rights movement that had come to see the great Frank Williams Sr. before he was put in his final resting place. He was a remarkable man who had touched the lives of many people, both black and white. Big Daddy had participated in various marches. He helped to fight against segregation, and he was also a supporter of women's rights. Therefore, many women activists from all over the country attended his funeral.

Big Mama and the rest of the family had determined that their church would not be big enough to hold all of the people who were going to attend the funeral. They decided to have his funeral at a historical black park. Finally, it was time for the funeral. It had seemed as if Sunday would never come. Big Mama had been up all morning listening to gospel music and preparing breakfast. Now that she had finished breakfast, it was time for her to wake up the rest of the family so that they could eat. It had been years since the whole family had spent a night at home. The Williams family house was a five-bedroom, two-bathroom house. Everyone shared a room: Marcus and Maurice, Black and Pam, Frank and Ms. Johnson, Left and Maria, and Big Mama and Truce. Big Mama went to the bedroom doors and announced that it was breakfast. After every one ate, the women helped clean up the kitchen. Then they all got ready for the funeral.

Big Mama seemed to be disturbed. Maybe it was just the funeral. After all, the only man in the world that she had ever loved was gone. He'd left her with two sons, three grandchildren, and forty-five years of pure love. She had been fifteen and he had been sixteen when they'd married. They were both born in Selma, Alabama, and they'd lived there as a young, happy family until Frank was born. Then they moved to Detroit for about five years. After Black was born, Big Daddy moved to Chicago, but on occasions he would return to Alabama to help protest and fight against segregation.

"Big Mama, Big Mama!"

"Yes, Truce?"

"The limousines are out here."

"Okay, baby. Let me get my purse."

After Big Mama got her purse, the Williams family loaded up in the limousines. It took about two hours to get to the park where the funeral was to be held. There were about a hundred cars in line; this was why it took so long to get to the park. The funeral was very sad. Frank took Big Daddy's death very hard. As a matter of fact, all of the family shed tears, except for Truce and Big Mama. It seemed as if Truce and Big Mama were trying to hold up for each other. There had to be at least fifteen hundred people at the funeral. Big Mama was given about five plaques from different organizations. There were many people who spoke words of encouragement to the Williams family. Instead of mourning over Big Daddy's death, the people who were close to him celebrated his life and the life that he gave to others. What was supposed to be a funeral turned out to be a family reunion.

After the funeral was over, the Williams family returned to the family house. Black and Frank tried to get Big Mama to stay with them until she got over the loss of Big Daddy. No matter how hard you try, when you lose a loved one, the loss never really fades away. You simply have to learn how to deal with it. After Black took Left and Maria to the bus station, Big Mama ran Frank and Ms. Johnson home. Now it was only Big Mama and Truce at the house. Big Mama put on some blues. Truce tried to stay up so that she could watch over Big Mama, but Big Mama reminded Truce that she had to go school in the morning.

Truce went to bed. While looking at the ceiling, thoughts of Big Daddy set in even harder in the back of her head. She remembered when Big Daddy used to push her in the swing as if it were yesterday. He used to take her to the park and buy her ice-cream cones. Big Daddy bought Truce her first bicycle when she was seven years old. Truce smiled as tears ran down her face. She thought about the times when Big Daddy used to sneak her candy after Big Mama had told her she couldn't have any. Big Daddy's presence around the house was definitely going to be missed. There wouldn't be anybody around the house to threaten to ground her for ten years and take away her car.

Her chain of thought was broken after she heard crying coming from the living room. She got out of her bed and rushed into the living room. Sure enough, Big Mama was sitting on the couch, crying. Finally Big Mama let out all of the hurt and tears that she had held in at the funeral. Truce ran to Big Mama and put her arms around her. Big Mama was shivering and shaking.

"Big Mama, it's going to be all right."

"He's gone, baby. He's gone! My Frank is gone, and he's not coming back. Frank, don't leave me! Please don't leave me!" screamed Big Mama as she and Truce embraced each other on the couch.

CHAPTER 19

Over the next couple of months, Big Mama went through many changes after Big Daddy's death. However, she and Truce grew even closer. Their relationship as grandmother and granddaughter evolved to a new level, and they were now like sisters.

As for Truce, she began to take her relationship with Eric more seriously. They were even talking about marrying after she graduated from law school. Eric was the love of her life; she would give anything in the world to spend eternity with him.

It was time for her and Eric to attend the senior prom, even though Eric had been out of school for nearly two years. Truce had impatiently waited for this day. The only thing that bothered her was she didn't know what kind of dress or color she was going to wear. This was a job for Big Mama. If there was one thing that Big Mama knew about besides cooking and history, it was how to dress.

After Truce made it home from school, she decided to ask Big Mama to help her pick out a prom dress. "Big Mama, I need your help. I need you to help me pick out something sharp to wear to the prom."

"Okay, baby. We need to get to the mall before it closes," replied Big Mama.

While they drove to and from the mall, Truce thought about Eric and the prom. There was no reason for her to be nervous. Asia was going to be there, right by her side. As for Imani, she was in

Los Angeles attending medical school. Tonight would be a very special night. After Truce and Big Mama returned from the mall with Truce's prom dress, Truce began to prepare for the prom.

Big Mama walked into the living room with cotton between her toes and said, "Okay, baby girl. I see that you have painted your toenails, yes?"

"And I need you to paint my fingernails."

"Girl, hand me that towel in your hand and that fingernail polish, and have a seat on the couch. So, baby girl, tell me: do you plan on doing something with Eric?"

"No, ma'am! Eric and I have agreed to wait until we are married before we have any more sex."

"Baby girl, I didn't ask you what you planned on doing when you and Eric get married. I asked you if you have any protection."

"No, ma'am."

"Hold up, baby girl," said Big Mama as she got up from the couch and walked into another room. She soon returned from her room. "Here, baby girl. You do know what these are, don't you?"

"Yes, ma'am. I'm eighteen years old."

"That's not what I asked you. I know how old you are. You are my granddaughter—I used to change your diapers. I was there when you took your first steps. I'm the first person that you peed on."

Upon hearing this, Truce laughed. "I didn't know that I used to bathroom on you."

"You sure did. The first time that I babysat you, you showered me in the middle of my favorite soap opera. I missed the rest of my soap opera because I had to stop and change you right on the couch. You had the prettiest smile on your face. It seemed as if you peed on me just to get my attention."

"Well, did I get your attention?"

"Baby, you have had my attention ever since I laid eyes on you. After Frank, I couldn't have any more kids. I have always wished for a daughter. God sent you to me. Frank used to say that I was overprotective of you. Your mother and father said that I took you away from them. Okay, baby girl, you didn't answer my question."

"Big Mama, what did you ask me?"

"Do you know what this is?"

"Yes, ma'am. It's a condom."

"Do you know how it is used?"

"Yes, it is placed on the penis in order to stop semen from entering the vagina. It is used to help prevent pregnancy and sexually transmitted diseases."

"Baby girl, you are exactly right. I'm too young to be a great-grandmother."

Truce burst into laughter.

Someone knocked on the door, and Big Mama looked through the peephole in the door. "It's Eric," she said.

"Big Momma, don't open the door," Truce aid as she hurried to her room, closing the door behind her.

Big Mama opened the door. "Hey, Eric. Come in, baby."

"Big Mama, how are you doing?"

"Fine."

"If I was a few years younger, I would be chasing you all over Chicago."

"Well, son, if I was thirty-five years younger, you wouldn't have to chase me because I would be running to you! Have a seat, Eric. Truce will be out in a minute. So how's your mother doing?"

"She is doing fine."

"Truce tells me that you are planning on getting married when she gets out of law school."

"Yes, ma'am. She is making me wait. I wanted to marry her after her graduation."

"Well, baby, you don't want to rush into anything. Marriage costs, especially when you start having children. You need to be financially stable."

"Yes, ma'am, you are right."

"Just have patience, Eric. By the time that Truce graduates from law school, she will be able to get a job with a salary big enough to buy a house as big as this one, if not bigger and you should have enough money saved up to support the both of you until Truce's job starts rolling."

Truce entered the living room wearing a sky blue dress with light blue shoes. As for Eric, he had on a black double-breasted suit, white shirt, black tie, black shoes, and a black derby hat.

"Truce, you look so beautiful!"

"Thank you, Eric. You are sharp too!"

"Well, I try to do my best," Eric said with a smile.

Someone knocked at the door. "Eric, get the door while I grab my camera." Eric opened the door. Pam screamed as she and Black walked through the door. Pam put a big kiss on the side of Eric's face.

"Daddy!" screamed Truce as she hugged Black.

"Baby girl, you look beautiful," Black said. "Now, where's Big Mama?"

"Here I am. Now, let me take a picture of y'all," Big Mama said with the camera in her hand.

"Hold up," Pam said as she hugged Black, Truce, and Eric while they posed for the camera. After Big Mama snapped the first picture, she handed Black the camera so that he could take a picture of her with Truce and Eric. After they had used up all of the film in their camera, Truce and Eric departed, heading to the prom.

Truce sat quietly in the car. "What's up, honey?" Eric said. "You have been quiet ever since we left the house."

"I'm just thinking about Imani. I wish that she could be here for the prom."

"Truce, she's probably busy."

"Yes, I talked to her last night. She told me that she wasn't going to make it to the prom because she had a big test coming up, but she promised me that she would be at my graduation."

"Well, Truce, we are here," Eric said as they pulled into the school parking lot. The lot was full of students.

Truce spotted Asia sitting on the hood of her blue 1987 Fifth Avenue. "Asia, Asia!" screamed Truce as she closed the car door behind her.

Asia came across the parking lot to meet Truce. "Hey, baby girl," Asia said as they embraced. "Truce, girl, you sharp as a tack."

"Thank you, girl. Big Mama helped me pick this dress."

"Big Mama still knows how to put a set of rags together. Hey, Eric," Asia said to Eric as he walked up.

"So I guess you're not going to give me a hug?" Eric said to Asia.

"You know that you are my brother-in-law, Eric," said Asia as she hugged Eric.

Eric put his arm around Truce and Asia as they headed toward the gymnasium. They heard loud music was coming from gym. After they entered, Truce received a hug and a kiss from her brother Marcus.

"Baby girl," said Marcus, "you have grown up right before my eyes. Sooner or later, you are going to make me an uncle, but you will always be my little sister. Eric, you take care of my baby sister."

"Marcus, you don't have to worry about anything. I am protecting her with my life."

"That's good. Then I won't have to take your life," Marcus said as he walked away with four of his boys.

"Marcus, you don't run my life," yelled Truce.

Eric said, "That's all right, honey. He's just trying to protect you."

"I don't need him to protect me. I have you to protect me."

Asia said, "Girl, that damn Marcus is a straightforward ass brother. He speaks what's on his mind."

"He needs to mind his own business."

"You're his baby sister."

"I know, Asia, but I'm eighteen years old and on my way to law school. Marcus can't keep being overprotective of me."

"Honey, I am going to speak to some of my brothers."

"Okay, Eric. I will be all right here with Asia."

"Girl, let's get a seat. My feet are tired."

"Okay, Asia."

Asia and Truce sat down. Shortly after, they started talking.

The one girl who wanted Eric just as much as Truce did walked up with five girls. Rholanda said, "Hey, Truce."

"Rholanda, girl, you are clean as hell. I love that dress."

"Thank you. Where's Eric?"

"He went to see how many of his boys came to the prom."

"Well, Truce I will see you around," Rholanda said as she walked away with a small clique of girls.

"I don't like that bitch," said Asia.

"Tell me about it, girl," replied Truce.

Truce and Asia sat at the table for hours. It was almost time for the prom to be over. Asia noted, "Damn, baby girl. Eric must have gotten lost. He has been gone for a long time."

As they held a conversation at the table, one of Asia's friends, Cleo, approached their table. "Excuse me, girl," Cleo said to Asia. "I need to give you some information."

"Shit, what are you waiting on? Excuse me, Truce. I'll be right back." Shortly after, Asia and Cleo returned, and Asia had a frown on her face. "Come on, baby girl."

"Asia, what's the matter?"

"Cleo says that she saw Eric and Rholanda go into one of the classrooms."

"What?"

"Yeah, and Cleo says the lights were off. They might still be in there."

"Take me to the classroom."

When they came to the classroom, sure enough, the lights were off. "This is the one," Cleo said.

Truce, Asia, and Cleo entered the classroom quietly without turning on the lights. They could hear a light moan coming from the back of the classroom.

Asia whispered to Cleo, "Find the light switch. When I tell you, turn on the lights." Truce and Asia walked to the back of the classroom, and the moaning got louder as they approached. When they looked behind the desk, they saw two people on the floor having sex. Cleo turned on the lights. Eric was lying between Rholanda's legs.

"Eric, how could you?" said Truce. "How could you cheat on me with this bitch?"

"Hold up, Truce. I can explain."

"Who are you calling a bitch?" said Rholanda.

"She's calling you a bitch, and if you don't like what my little sister said, you can take it up with me!" Asia said as she rolled her head and neck while putting her hands on her hips.

"No, Asia. I can fight my own battles," Truce said as she took off her high heels. "You want some of me, bitch?"

Eric stepped between her and Rholanda. "Honey, let me talk to you."

"Eric, get your damn hands off me."

"You heard my little sister. Now, get your damn hands off her before I cut your ass from A to Z."

"Bitch, you don't have nothing to do with this."

"Eric, what's up, nigger? Let's dance," said Asia as she pulled out a straight razor.

"Let me handle this," said Marcus as he approached them. Someone must have gotten Marcus because he had three guys with him. Marcus looked at his baby sister, whose eyes was full of tears. "Baby girl, what's the matter?"

"Marcus, it's just a misunderstanding," Eric said.

"Eric, I'm not talking to you. And by the way, take your hands off my sister. Okay, baby girl, now tell big brother what's the matter."

"Eric and this bitch were having sex in here, and I caught them."

"Eric, didn't I tell you to not hurt my sister?" Marcus punched Eric in the face, and the two tied up.

Truce slapped Rholanda, and they began to fight. Asia hit Rholanda in the back of the head. Then Cleo grabbed Asia. "Let her fight, Asia."

"Cleo, that's my little sister."

"She has to learn how to stand on her own. Truce is a big girl—she can handle herself."

Truce and Rholanda fought while Marcus and his friends stomped Eric. As Truce and Rholanda fought, Rholanda began to back away from Truce, but she didn't stop swinging. Then she slipped and fell. Truce jumped on top of her and punched her in the face.

"Whip her ass, baby girl!" screamed Asia as Truce beat Rholanda in the face.

Marcus looked over and saw Truce on top of Rholanda, beating her. By this time, Eric was unconscious. Marcus walked over and pulled Truce off Rholanda.

"Marcus, let me go!" screamed Truce.

"Come on, baby girl. You can't be jumping on people. That's not ladylike. Besides, Dad would kill me if he knew that I allowed you to fight. Now, let's go before Uncle Frank's girlfriend comes in here and sees us."

Marcus and his friends escorted Truce, Asia, and Cleo out of the school and into the parking lot. "Asia, you take Truce home just in case I get pulled over by the cops. I know that someone is going to tell the security guard my name."

"Okay, Marcus. I will make sure that she gets home safe. Come on, baby girls. Let's go before the police come."

Marcus opened the passenger door of Asia's car for Truce. She got in, and Marcus gave her a kiss on the forehead before closing the door. "I love you, little sister."

"I love you too, Marcus."

As Asia pulled out of the student parking lot, the police passed by them with their sirens on.

CHAPTER 20

Over the next months, Truce hardened her heart toward all men. She didn't even have a date for graduation. Imani and Asia tried to encourage their sister that she could date other guys and that all guys were not like Eric, but Truce refused to date any of the guys trying to get with her. She spent nearly the whole summer in the house around Big Mama. The only time that she left the house was to visit her mother, her father, and Asia, and to take Big Mama where she needed to go.

Imani called from California to check on Truce. Imani had found a job at a hospital in Los Angeles after she graduated from medical school, and she moved there.

Eric had been trying to make it up to Truce, but it was to no avail because she was a woman who had been scorned.

It was now time for Truce to go to law school. Her family and friends decided to throw her a going-away party. "Truce, Truce," Big Mama called. "I need for you to go to the store for me and pick up some things."

"Okay, Big Mama."

Big Mama handed her a long list of things.

Truce looked at the list of things. "We must be really low on food."

"Yes, baby girl."

"Okay, I will see you when I get back."

After Truce walked out the door, Big Mama got on the phone and called friends and family who had planned to throw Truce a party. Asia was already at the grocery store, waiting on Truce so that she could get Truce in a conversation long enough for Big Mama, Pam, Imani, and the rest to set up everything.

After Truce made it to the grocery store, she noticed that Asia's blue Regal was in the parking lot. She said to herself, *At least I will have someone to talk to.* As Truce entered the grocery store, she spotted Asia pushing a grocery cart. She grabbed a cart and headed toward Asia. "Asia!" Truce hollered.

"Hey, girl, what's up? What are you doing here? Are you following me?"

"No, Big Mama sent me here to buy us half of the grocery store."

"Girl, quit playing."

"If you think I'm lying, check out this grocery list," Truce said as she handed the list to Asia.

"Damn, baby girl. Big Mama must be planning a big dinner for Sunday."

"I don't know what's she's planning. The only thing that I do know is this is a lot of damn food." They laughed at Truce's statement.

"Truce, I am going to trail you to the house so that I can help you with groceries. Besides, I need to see Big Mama; it has been almost two weeks since I've visited." After Truce bought everything that Big Mama had requested and the bag boy put the grocery bags in the car for her, Truce headed to the house while Asia trailed her.

When Truce made it to the house, she opened the door and grabbed a grocery bag, Asia also got a bag from the back seat of Truce's car, and they walked to the door. Truce knocked on the door, but Big Mama didn't come to the door. "Big Mama must be next door," said Truce as she unlocked the door with her key.

As Truce entered the house, she was met with loud voices. "Surprise! Surprise, baby girl!" Maurice hugged his little sister.

"I thought you were in Germany, Maurice!"

"Where's my hug?" Uncle Frank said.

"Don't leave me out," said Uncle Left.

The Williams family had a great time. Although it was Truce's going-away party, it was just like a family reunion because friends and family members came from far and near to attend. After all, her life and name represented unity between two local street organizations that often had bloodbaths over street corners and turf that neither of them owned.

CHAPTER 21

Truce thought about her friends and family members as she sat on the bus. Though Eric had broken her heart and turned her against all men, she thought about him. After all, he was the one who had taken her virginity, and he was her first love. No one knew her in Washington, DC, and therefore she would have a fresh start. Although Washington was predominately black and there would be a lot of handsome brothers there, her mind was made up. Her reason for coming to Washington was to attend law school, not to be hurt by another boy posing as a man.

Truce fell asleep; she had been riding the bus for hours, and she was tired. The bus driver announced to the passengers, "We are now entering Washington, DC. We will be stopping at a resting area in about twenty minutes."

Truce was awakened by the bus driver's voice coming through the intercom. As she looked through the window, she smiled after seeing the sign that read, "Welcome to Washington." Shortly after the bus passed the sign, she was able to see another sign that read, "Bus stop ahead."

"We will be here at this bus stop for about forty-five minutes. Passengers who are coming to Washington, DC, may exit here. Those of you who want to get off for refreshments or to stretch, remember to be back here in forty-five minutes. It is now five fifteen; try to be back by six o'clock, no later than six fifteen."

Truce grabbed her two suitcases and exited the bus. The bus stop was bigger that the bus stop in Chicago. It had a Burger King and a McDonald's. She was hungry after riding for hours from Chicago to Washington, DC. After Truce peeped through the glass doors of the bus station at the restaurants, she decided to enter and head straight to the McDonald's.

"May I help you?" said the young white woman behind the counter.

"Yes, I would like a double cheeseburger, a large fries, and a strawberry drink."

"How about an apple pie?"

"I will take a fudge sundae."

The woman added up everything. "That will cost four dollars and twenty-seven cents." Truce paid the woman for her meal and took a seat.

After she finished eating, Truce went outside to catch a cab to the university. There were several cabs parked outside. Truce walked over to a cab at random and found out the driver was a middle aged black woman. "Excuse me, sister," Truce said to the cab driver.

"Yes, I'm waiting on you. Where are we headed?" said the woman as she got out of the cab, opened up the trunk, and put Truce's suitcases inside.

"Washington State," answered Truce after they got back into the cab.

"Okay. You going to college?"

"Yes."

"What are to going to take up?"

"Criminology and law."

"You must be planning on becoming a lawyer."

"Well, sort of. I plan on becoming a district attorney."

"I'm sorry," said the driver. "I didn't even introduce myself. My name is Ann, but everyone calls me Cookie. I am originally from Detroit."

"My name is Truce. I'm from Chicago."

"The Windy City?"

"Yes, I'm afraid so."

"How long does it take to become a district attorney?"

"About seven or eight years, but I plan on going to school all year round, so it should take me about four and a half years. I have been studying law ever since I was in the eighth grade. I was fortunate to take the bar test earlier this year, and I passed it. I am able to pass the bar right now, but I am going to get some experience, so in about seven or eight years, I should be on the payroll."

"What made you want to become a district attorney?"

"I'm tired of these white-collar criminals getting off. The petty criminals always take the fall."

Ann said, "Well, little sister, that's good. We need some more of us inside the legal system. Besides, the judicial system is destroying all of the black men."

"This must be the university?"

"Yes, girl, this is it."

Truce and Ann got out of the car. Ann opened up the trunk and took out Truce's suitcases. "It has been a pleasure meeting you, Truce."

"No, Ann, it has been a pleasure meeting you. How much do I owe you?"

"The meter reads thirty-two dollars and twenty-five cents, but give me ten dollars—that will be enough."

"No, Ann. I have enough money to pay you."

"Truce don't turn down gifts anytime someone offers you one. Some people give because it makes them feel good. Hold up for one minute, li'l' sister, before you go." Ann got a small piece of paper from the car. She wrote on the paper and handed it to Truce. "Here's my home number. If there's anything that I can do to help you while you are here in DC, just call me."

"Okay, thank you, Ann," Truce said as she hugged the woman.

"I must be going, Truce. I am missing a lot of money. I have a daughter who will be going to college in four years, and I want to put some money away for her." Ann got into the car and drove away.

Truce picked up her suitcases, took a deep breath, and said to herself, *My key is on the other side of that door.* Then she walked through the door marked "Main Office."

As she entered, a black woman stood behind a counter that had a sign on top of it. "May I help you?" said the woman.

"Yes, ma'am. My name is Truce Williams. I was given a full scholarship to this college. This is my first day."

"Okay," said the woman as she sat down at a computer. "Your name is Truce Williams? Here it is: Truce Kayla Williams. You are from Chicago?"

"Yes, ma'am."

"You have a full scholarship?" The woman got up and handed Truce some papers. "Sign these registration papers. When you get through, a student aid will show you to your dorm."

"I'm finished," Truce said, holding her registration papers in her hand. The woman took the papers out of Truce's hand. Then she turned to a student who was sitting at a table and said, "Show her where she needs to go."

The student got up and said to Truce, "Hello," extending her hand. Truce shook it. "My name is Angela."

"My name is Truce."

"It's a pleasure to meet you, Truce. Let me get one of those suitcases for you."

"Thank you."

They walked out of the main office, Truce following Angela's lead. Angela was a short white girl with a body like a runway model. She was slim, had brown eyes, and had long light brown hair. "So, Truce, where you from?"

"I'm from Chicago."

"I'm from San Diego. My parents are in the military. They made me go to college. So far, I like it. There are a lot of handsome guys here. You will like it."

"Well, Angela, I didn't come here to meet a guy. I just got out of a bad relationship."

"I have a friend from Louisiana that you might like." Truce looked at Angela with a smile on her face. Angela returned the smile and added, "He's black."

"Sorry, Angela. I'm still not interested."

"Girl, he's sexy. Would you at least meet him?"

"I haven't been here twenty-four hours. Let me get myself settled in first, and then I might think about it."

"His name's Alamin." Angela looked at a card in her hand. "You are going to Jill Hall, room fifty-two. Jill Hall is right across this sidewalk. There's the cafeteria over there. Also, there are two restaurants, a coffee shop, and a movie theater. The mall is in walking distance, and so is the grocery store."

"I think that I am going to like this college life," said Truce.

"Jill Hall," announced Angela as she and Truce walked through the door.

"Hey, Angela," said a dark-skinned girl sitting at a small desk.

"Hey, Carol. This is Truce; she's from Chicago."

"Pleased to meet you, Truce. You are going to like it here. So what room are you in?"

"I'm in room fifty-two."

"That's my room. Angela, let me take that suitcase. I will show her to the room, and I will also show her around campus."

"Okay," Angela said. "Truce, I am going to leave you with Carol. I will see you later."

"Thank you, Angela."

"You're welcome."

As they walked up some stairs, Carol asked Truce, "What are you planning to get a degree in?"

"Criminology."

"You must be planning on being a lawyer. Girl, if I was to become a district attorney, I would have to lock up all of my brothers and homies. Breaking the law has become a way of life for them."

"I know the feeling—I have three brothers. One of them, Maurice, is in the military. Marcus is a disciple, and I have another brother, Bobby, who's a vice lord. Girl, he has been getting locked up ever since I was five years old. As a matter of fact, he's locked up now." Both girls burst into laughter. "One thing about it, girl: he's very cute. All of my brothers are heartbreakers."

"Do you have any pictures of them?"

"Yes, I have pictures of all of them."

"Girl, I know that you are going to show me those pictures."

Truce promised, "When I get myself situated, I will show them to you."

"This is our room," said Carol as she removed the key from her front pocket and opened the door. Truce and Carol walked into the room.

Truce scanned the room. "Carol, I see that you have a lot of Afrocentric pictures on the wall."

"Yes, I come from a very cultural background. This is your bed." Carol pointed at a bed that had a pillow on it with no pillowcase. "The sheets are in these two drawers. The pillowcases are in here, the blankets are in here, and here's your key to the room. Whatever's in the refrigerator is yours."

The phone rang, and Carol picked it up. "Hello? Angela, what's up, girl? Yes, we are coming to the cafeteria. She's right here—we just walked through the door. Truce, it's Angela."

Truce took the phone. "Hello? Yeah. Girl, I just got here—I don't want to talk to no man. What? No, you didn't! I guess you are going to do your own thing regardless of what I say. All right, bye."

"What did Carol want?"

"She has some brother named Alamin that she wants me to meet."

"Girl, you are going to like him, He's probably the finest man on the whole campus. Tall and dark-skinned with the body of a Zulu warrior."

"Well, Carol, I'm not looking for a relationship right now. I just got out of a bad relationship."

"He's a nice brother."

"Then why don't you take him?" Truce countered.

"I'm engaged already. If I wasn't, I would use every trick that my mama taught me to try to get him. But anyway, put your suitcases on the bed. It's time to go to the cafeteria for dinner. You can put your things up when we get back."

CHAPTER 22

Months quickly passed. Truce had promised herself that she would never let another man get next to her heart, but she couldn't help herself. Alamin was winning her over. He was strong and very confident in himself. Like her, Alamin wanted to help reshape black America. Unlike her previous boyfriend, Eric, Alamin was mature and didn't force himself on her.

Truce was in English class, math class, and every other class thinking of Alamin. Should she go on a date with Alamin? The date was scheduled for tonight. The bell rang, and school was out until Monday. Truce made her way to the door with the rest of the students. She was greeted by Alamin with a smile in the hallway.

"Truce, what's up?"

"Nothing much, just a little tired. What's up with you, Alamin?"

"Well, it depends on if you let me take you out to the movies."

"I guess it wouldn't hurt to go out with you. Besides, you seem like a real brother."

"I will be over to pick you up at seven o'clock."

"Okay, I will be waiting for you."

Carol walked up while Truce and Alamin were talking. "What's up, Alamin?" Carol said.

"Just chillin'."

"Alamin, you like my girl, don't ya?"

"Carol, don't go there," said Truce.

"Yeah, I like her. I cannot lie."

"You and my girl will make a good couple."

Truce said, "Come on, Carol. Let's go before you say too much."

"I will see you, Truce, at seven o'clock."

"Okay, Alamin," Truce said as she and Carol walked out of the school.

"Truce, why didn't you tell me that you and Alamin were getting close?"

"We are just going out."

"Yeah, right. I know that you are going to let Alamin get it."

"Get what?"

"You know what I'm talking about."

"I don't have sex with a man on our first date. Well, I'm getting me some tonight from my fiancé."

"That's different—you are having sex with a man you are planning to marry in nine months."

"Okay, I'm sorry, Truce. I was just trying to help. I didn't mean any harm."

"Carol, I know that you didn't mean any harm. If Alamin shows me that he's worthy, don't worry—I am going to put it on him."

Both Truce and Carol burst into laughter.

"Girl, give me some skin," said Carol. She and Truce gave each other five. The girls entered their dormitory and headed to their room. When they entered, the phone began to ring.

Truce answered the phone. "Hello? What's up, girl? Yeah, she's right here getting ready for tonight, putting her clothes on the bed. I know that you are not going to wear that. Angela, you need to get over here and see this leather miniskirt. Ha! Carol, Angela asked if you have an extra miniskirt she can borrow for tonight."

"Tell her yeah," said Carol.

"Angela, Carol says that she has one for you. Okay, Angela, I will talk to you later. Bye." Truce hung up and turned to Carol. "Girl, what was Angela talking about?"

"That's one crazy white girl. She has to have some sista in her somewhere. Truce, you know that her best friend she grew up with is black."

"I didn't know that. No wonder she's so down on everything."

"Well, girl I am going to take my bath. Jerome is going to swing by here early to pick me up. I won't be back until Sunday, so you and Alamin can have the room to yourselves."

While Carol was in the bathroom taking a bath, Jerome came over. Truce talked to Jerome until Carol came out of the bathroom dressed.

"Hey, baby."

"Hey, Jerome."

"You ready to go?" Jerome asked.

"Yes. Here's my bag."

Jerome picked up the blue nylon bag. Truce walked to the door with Carol and Jerome. Carol and Truce hugged before Carol and Jerome left.

Truce looked at the clock on the wall: it was five thirty. *Alamin will be over here in about an hour.* Truce undressed, put a towel around her, and headed to the bathroom to shower. Thirty minutes later, she walked out of the bathroom, sat on the bed, and put lotion on her body. After that, she put on a yellow sun dress and a yellow pair of sandals. Next, she stood in front of the mirror and checked herself out. Then she opened up the closet and took out her yellow purse, which matched her dress and shoes.

Someone knocked on the door. *It must be Alamin,* she said to herself. Truce opened the door, and sure enough it was Alamin. He came in.

"Girl, you sure look good."

"Thank you, Alamin. You are no slouch yourself, looking like an African king."

"Well, being able to have a chance to take you out makes me feel like a king."

"Keep talking, brother. I just love flattery."

"Whatever you love, precious, is what I love."

"I hear you with all that talk, brother, but time will tell."

"Are you ready to go, Truce?"

Truce and Alamin walked out of the door. As they walked to the parking lot, Alamin said, "Come on, Truce. My car is right over here." He led Truce to a black BMW that was parked by a blue truck. Then he walked to the passenger side and opened the door. Truce got in. Alamin closed the door for her, walked around to the driver's side, and got in.

"I like your car, Alamin."

"I have had this car for two years. My dad promised to buy me a Mercedes-Benz and another house if I come back to New Orleans and run the family business."

"You have a house?"

"Yes, I have a three-bedroom house in Baton Rouge."

"What kind of business does your family run?"

"Well, it depends. My mother owns a chain of beauty salons. My father has several stores: seven fast food restaurants, two five-star restaurants, three night clubs, one jazz club, a chain of barber shops, and three car lots. That's not including my two brothers' businesses, and my own restaurant and two flea markets."

"Your family must be a part of the Mafia," Truce said with a smile on her face.

"You know, I've never looked at it like that in the twenty-two years I have been living." Truce and Alamin laughed.

Alamin turned into a parking lot that had a big sign with lights on it, and it read, "Old Times." Alamin parked the car. "This is a jazz restaurant, and I come here often. They serve good soul food," he said as he opened up the restaurant door for Truce.

"Do you have a reservation?"

"Yes. Alamin Johnson."

The man dressed in a black tuxedo flipped through a reservation book. "Okay, here it is: Alamin Johnson, reservation for two. Let me show you to your table." The man led them to a table in the corner. The man pulled out Truce's seat for her.

"Thank you, sir."

"You're welcome." The waiter handed them both menus. "Let me know when you are ready to place your order," he said as he walked away from their table.

Alamin and Truce looked at their menus. "Truce, have you decided what you want to order?"

"I'm thinking about trying this shrimp gumbo, fried okra, red beans, and apple pie with a glass of lemonade."

"I have never eaten any shrimp gumbo."

Truce said, "You don't know what you are missing. My mother cooks shrimp gumbo all the time—it's really good. Waiter, waiter!"

"Yes, ma'am?"

"I'm ready to place my order. I want to try the shrimp gumbo, fried okra, red beans, apple pie, and a glass of lemonade."

The waiter wrote down Truce's order. "What will you be having, sir?"

"Just give me whatever she's having."

"Yes, sir. Your orders will be ready shortly."

"Alamin, you ordered the same thing that I ordered."

"I told you: whatever you like, I like."

After Truce and Alamin finished eating, Alamin paid the bill and then drove them to his apartment. Truce looked at all of the pictures of black heroes that covered the walls in the living room of Alamin's apartment. The furniture was even black in Alamin's apartment.

"Alamin, I see that you are very fond of the black heroes."

"Yeah, precious. I'm all about helping in the uplifting of black people."

"Well, that's one thing that we do have in common. I am all about helping my people. Now, this is my girl right here. Assatha

Shakur! She's my idol. Assatha Shakur represents the courage of the black woman."

Alamin walked over to the stereo and searched through a stack of CDs. He found a CD of Al Green's, put it into the disc player, walked over to a switch, and turned it on. The room filled with red light as Al Green's voice flowed through the speakers. "Truce, would you like to dance?" he asked.

Truce responded with a smile, "Brother, I thought you would never ask."

"I didn't want to move too fast," Alamin said as he embraced Truce. They stared into each other's eyes and slowly danced as Al Green's voice set the tone in the room. They smiled at each other. Alamin placed a light kiss on Truce's forehead. Next, he parted her lips with his tongue. Truce's heart began to beat fast. Alamin put his hand up the back of Truce's shirt and unfastened her bra. Alamin then pulled her shirt up until Truce's breast was exposed. Her nipples were hard and very erect. He took one of her breasts into his mouth. Truce let out another moan. Her feet felt very light, and she found it very difficult to remain standing on her feet while Alamin performed foreplay on her in the middle of the floor. Alamin picked Truce up and walked her into his bedroom. Alamin laid Truce on the bed and unbuttoned her shirt as Truce unbuttoned his shirt. Then she began to help Alamin out of his pants. It wasn't that Alamin needed any help to remove his pants, but he was taking too long for her, and her tolerance level had dropped to zero.

After their clothes were removed, his erection excited her even more. Truce pulled Alamin's organ in an up-and-down motion.

"Oh, baby," moaned Alamin. He thought that he was going to burst. Truce wrapped her legs around Alamin's waist. She slid back on the bed as Alamin entered her sacred chamber with a slow, gentle, deep thrust. Not only did Alamin fill her up with his shaft, but he had a few inches left—more than she had ever experienced before. Alamin was the second guy in her life she had had sex with.

Alamin was very experienced in this field, and therefore he was very gentle with her. Alamin sped up the pace as he neared his peak. Alamin let a deep moan as he exploded inside of Truce. This also brought on her climax, and she pulled him deeper into her. Alamin rolled over on his back. Truce laid her head on his chest and looked Alamin in the face with tears in her eyes that ran down her face.

"What's the matter, precious?" said Alamin as he wiped the tears away from her face with his hand.

"Please don't hurt me," replied Truce. "I promised myself that I would never allow another man the chance to hurt me again."

Alamin stared deeply into Truce's big, pretty brown eyes and said, "I'm not here to hurt you. My desire is only to comfort and love you."

With that statement Truce was comfortable. The two fell asleep, tired from a night of ecstasy.

CHAPTER 23

Although three years had passed since Truce and Alamin had gotten together and they were now engaged to get married in nine months, it seemed like only yesterday when they'd met.

Truce was awakened by the phone. Before she could get her vision together, Carol handed her the phone. Truce thought to herself as she took the phone from Carol, *Who could be calling me this early in the morning?*

"Hello? Hey, Big Mama, what's up? For real? What's wrong with her? How long has she known that she's had it? She looked fine the last time that I saw her. Oh, yes, ma'am. After I take a shower, I will go to the airport." Truce hung up the phone. "This can't be happening," she said as tears rolled down her face.

"What's the matter?" asked Carol.

"My sister Asia had to be rushed to the hospital the other night."

"What's wrong with her?"

"The doctor says that she has full-blown AIDS, with only a week left to live."

Upon hearing that, Carol put her arms around Truce.

Truce said, "That's my big sista. She said she was going to be at my graduation."

"Truce, you can't fall apart. Asia needs for you to be strong for her."

"I know, but she's supposed to be my maid of honor at my wedding in nine months." Truce picked up the phone and dialed.

"Who are you calling?"

"Alamin," answered Truce. "I've got to let him know that I have to go to Chicago to check on my sister. Honey, how are you doing?" she said to Alamin. "Something has come up, and I have to go home for a while. It's my big sister Asia—she's very sick, and the doctor has given her a week at the most to live. Big Mama says that she has full-blown AIDS. Oh, I have to take a shower. I'll see you when you get here. No, Alamin, honey, I will be fine. I know that you want to be there for me. Honey, I love you too. Bye." Truce hung up the phone.

"Girl, why don't you let Alamin go to Chicago with you?" Carol asked.

"I don't know."

"Now, Truce, you know that you two can't stand to be away from each other."

"I know," replied Truce as she put on her robe and headed to the shower. About fifteen minutes later, she returned from the bathroom and began to dress. After Truce was dressed, she started packing. Truce was very sharp. Everything that she had on was black. Truce wore a pair of black leather pants, a black leather vest, a black scarf, black shades, black leather boots, a black leather trench coat, and a pair of black leather gloves. Truce stood in front of the mirror that was on the dresser, admiring herself while waiting for Alamin to arrive.

There was a knock on the door; it had to be Alamin. Truce walked over to the door and opened it. Alamin entered the room with a concerned look on his face. He embraced Truce and kissed her deeply, parting her lips with his tongue. Truce's head began to spin, and she almost forgot that she had a plane to catch to Chicago in about an hour.

"Honey, I'm sorry about your sista," he said as gazed into Truce's brown eyes.

Truce stared back at him with a sad look on her face, like a child who had lost her favorite toy. Then she let out a sigh. "I guess that we should be going to the airport."

"Yes, I guess that you're right," said Alamin as he picked up Truce's two suitcases. The two exited Truce's room and headed to the parking lot. After they make it to the parking lot, Alamin put Truce's luggage in the trunk of his car and opened up the door on the passenger's side for her to get in. Alamin then got in the car and headed straight for the airport.

"Honey," Alamin said, "I thought that Carol is supposed to be moving out of the room with you."

"Yeah, she is moving in with her fiancé sometime this week."

"So when are you going to move in with me?"

"In a few months."

"How long is a few months?"

"After I graduate."

"That won't be for three months."

"Alamin, you sound as if I said three years."

"Precious, you know that I can't stand being without you."

"Alamin, you know that I feel the same way about you."

"Then why don't you let me come to Chicago with you?"

"Alamin, please don't make this any harder for me than it already is. My big sister is in the hospital dying, and I'm already stressed out."

"I'm sorry, precious," Alamin said as he turned into the airport. "We are here." He parked, got out, and walked around to the passenger's side of the car to open up the door for Truce.

Truce and Alamin entered the lobby of the airport. People seemed to be walking all over the place. Truce walked up to one of the counters and was greeted in a friendly way by a short, heavyset white man standing behind the counter. "Hello, ma'am! What can I do for you?"

"I was supposed to have a ticket wired here from my grandmother."

"What's your name?"

"Truce Williams."

"Hold up for a minute," said the man behind the counter. Then he walked over to a desk that had a computer on it. The man returned to the counter with a smile on his face. "Truce Kayla Williams."

"Yes, sir."

"May I see your ID?" Truce took her ID out of her purse and handed it to him. "Yes, ma'am. You have a round-trip ticket to Chicago. I need for you to put your signature right here."

After she signed for the ticket, her flight number was called over the intercom. "Honey, they are calling my flight," said Truce to Alamin.

The man behind the counter said, "Hold up, ma'am. Put this around the handles after you place your name on it, so that your luggage can be identified if you lose it."

Truce handed the tags to Alamin. "Honey, put these tags on my suitcases for me."

After Alamin put the tags on Truce's luggage, her flight number was called across the intercom again.

"Alamin, I have to go," Truce said as she kissed him gently on the lips. Then she picked up her suitcases and headed to a man who was checking people's luggage with a metal detector. After the man checked her suitcases, he allowed Truce to pass through. Alamin watched Truce from a distance as she exited through a door that led to her flight.

Truce fell asleep in her seat after the plane had been off the ground for about fifteen minutes.

CHAPTER 24

"Excuse me, ma'am," said a woman flight attendant, who also appeared to be one of the sisters who modeled for popular black magazines. "The plane is making a stop here in Chicago. Is this where you get off at or change planes? If not, you might want to get off and stretch your legs."

"Thank you," said Truce. "I must have been asleep for at least three hours. This is where I get off. I'm from Chi-town."

Truce picked up her luggage after she exited the plane. *I wonder who's coming to pick me up,* she thought as she sat on a bench outside the airport.

A white Mercedes-Benz with light tinted windows stopped in front of her bench. The window on the passenger's side rolled down slowly. "Need a ride?" said a voice from inside of the car.

Truce could recognize that voice from anywhere. "Big Mama!" she shouted.

Big Mama got out, and Imani got out of the driver's side of the car. The three women embraced one another outside of the airport; it was almost like a family reunion.

"Girl, look at you," said Imani to Truce. "You have put on about five pounds in your hips. Asia will be happy to see you." Imani opened the trunk of the car. "Let's put your luggage in here." After Truce put her suitcases in the trunk, she climbed in the back seat, and the three of them finished their conversation.

"So, Imani, is this your Mercedes-Benz?"

"Yeah. You like it?"

"Yeah, girl. It's very sharp. I plan on buying me one just like it after I get me a job. I want a black one."

"So, baby girl, tell us about this man that you have met at college."

"Oh, that's Alamin," said Truce with a smile on her face. "Okay, where do I begin?"

"Is he fine? Does he look good?" interjected Big Mama.

"Yeah, he's fine and looks good."

"Thank God!" said Big Mama. "I know that I taught you well. Don't bring no ugly men home—they make ugly children. And besides, there are only two ugly men in the world that I have been able to put up with, and those are your daddy and your uncle. I thank God for your two brothers. They have grown up to be two fine young men—one looks like Billy Dee Williams, and the other one looks like Duke Ellington. Now ain't that something?"

Imani and Truce burst into laughter. "Big Mama, you are still funny."

"What, you thought that I was going to lose my sense of humor? Child, please. Yesterday I was outside watering my flowers, and you should have heard those young men honking their horns. I had to go back in the house and take off my shorts. I nearly caused a nine-car collision." Truce and Imani laughed again at Big Mama's sense of humor.

"So, Truce, do you want to go home with Big Mama first, before you go to the hospital to see Asia? Or do you want to go to the hospital with me to see Asia?"

"I am going to the hospital with you."

"Big Mama, did you say that you wanted me to drop you back off at home?"

"Yes, I have some beans on, slow cooking."

Imani pulled up in the driveway of the house. "Big Mama, where's my car?" Truce asked.

"It's in the garage, baby girl." Big Mama got out of the car.

"Imani, wait for me. I am going to take my suitcases in the house, and then I am going to get my car and trail you to the hospital."

"Okay, baby girl."

Truce took her luggage into the house and kissed Big Mama on the cheek. Then she got her canary-yellow Eldorado Cadillac out of the garage and trailed Imani to the hospital.

After the two women parked their cars in the hospital's parking lot, they entered the hospital. Imani led the way to Asia's room as Truce followed closely beside her. Truce knocked on the door of Asia's room.

"Come in," said a voice from behind the door. Truce began to feel as if she were going to cry when she saw her sister lying in the hospital bed with IVs hooked up to her. Asia looked very weak, and she had lost about seventy pounds. Her eyes looked as if there were black rings around them. "Hey, baby girl," said Asia with a very weak voice. "Damn, I was wondering if I was going to see you again before I die."

"Stop saying that!" interjected Imani. "You are *not* going to die."

Truce walked over and leaned down to kiss Asia on the cheek. "Asia, I've missed you so much!"

"Girl, I missed you and Imani. So where are my two nieces?"

"They are at home with Mama."

"Can you still sing, baby girl?" Asia asked Truce.

"Yeah, I am still pretty good."

"I am very tired. How about singing me a few of those good old gospels?"

"If Imani will sing backup for me."

"For you, I will do it," said Imani.

Truce started off by singing Mahalia Jackson's "Precious Lord." By the time Truce had sung about four songs, a couple of nurses came into the room to listen to Truce's beautiful voice.

"Baby girl," said Asia, "won't you sing my favorite song?"

"What's that?"

"'Going Up Yonder,' girl."

"Okay," said Truce. "Imani, are you ready?"

"Yeah, girl, I guess so."

Truce began to sing. "If anyone should ask you where I am going soon, I beg you to tell them, to be with my Lord. I said I'm going up yonder, going up yonder!" As Truce and Imani sang Asia's favorite song, Asia fell into a deep sleep, never to awake again.

Printed in the United States
By Bookmasters